DANCE DANCE

Wherever You Might Be

J. F. LEAHY

M.R. QUINN

Naval Writers Group LLC

Annapolis – Newport – San Diego

DANCE DANCE WHEREVER YOU MIGHT BE

Photo Credit:

Cover Photo: Three Dancers

© 2018 iStockphoto LP by Getty Images, Calgary, Alberta, Canada

Photos of International Irish Dancing Associations following Chapter 1:

An Coimisiún le Rincí Gaelacha (CLRG) , *Used with permission*

ISBN: 069210867X

ISBN13: 9780692108673

Library Of Congress Control Nr. 2023861304

Naval Writers Group LLC, Annapolis MD

Dedication

To Erin and Pat,

Maura and Molly

Dance, then, wherever you may be,
I am the Lord of the Dance, said he,
And I'll lead you all, wherever you may be,
And I'll lead you all in the Dance, said he.

Sydney Carter

(c) 1963 Hope Publishing Company, Carol Stream,
Illinois 60188

(hope@hopepublishing.com)

Used With Permission

Acknowledgments

Although writing has been described as the loneliest of professions, no book is solely the work of the author listed on the cover. Thanks to the Naval Writers Group and others in helping to bring this work to fruition: and especially to my co-author M.R. Quinn, who knows vastly more about Irish Dancing and Irish Culture than I, and who actually can pronounce *Oireachtas* !

It is said that no man is a hero to his valet; neither is an author to his editor, especially an author whose grasp of the rules of punctuation is as tentative as mine. Thanks as always to Carolyn DiNovo, my long time editor for her skilled proof reading assistance. Cartons of gently used commas will soon appear for sale on E-bay.

TABLE OF CONTENTS

Author's Notes:

This is a work of fiction. The names, characters, governments, agencies, places, events, and incidents are either the products of the author's imagination or used in a fictitious manner. Any resemblance to actual persons, governments, agencies, nations, or officials living or dead, or actual events is purely coincidental.

Regarding the Cape Breton Miners Museum: Located on one of the most picturesque coasts of Cape Breton Island, on a 15-acre site filled with wild roses and grasses, the Cape Breton Miners Museum pays tribute to the region's long and rich history of coal mining. It is home to profound stories of miners and their families, and the resource that helped build a nation, and serves as the totally fictional location for this story.

Regarding the totally fictional Chechen "terrorists": While the co-authors understand the frustration of a people who are essentially voiceless and whose loss of their homeland has been long ignored by the international community, we do not endorse or support the use of violence in the resolution of this or any similar dispute.

CHAPTER ONE: DRIVEN TO SUCCEED

Erin Lincoln heard her alarm clock ringing at 4:00 AM. Groggily, she reached for her cell phone and silenced the alarm so that it would not wake her husband Pat, sleeping by her side. She laid back trying to gather her thoughts. "What am I doing awake at this hour, especially during Thanksgiving break?", she asked herself. "Why did I set that alarm?"

She laid there for just a few minutes until her mind cleared. "Ah, I know," she said. "Today's the day we take the girls down to suburban Philadelphia for the final qualifications for the 'Mid-Atlantic Regional Feis'. Today is the big one that the kids have been preparing for all season. If they make it here, they'll be on their way to the North American 'Grand Oireachtas' up in Nova Scotia. I'd better get a move on!"

After a quick shower and a cup of coffee, she returned to wake her husband. "Pat, you had better get up and get moving. We've got to get down to King of Prussia for the Mid-Atlantic Feis, and we need to be there to register no later than 9:30. And don't forget, we're taking Molly's new best friend from St. Margaret's school, little Angela Rossi, along with her parents, Don and Annamarie, so they can see what this Irish step dancing is all about. You remember Don. He's an executive at Global Pharmaceuticals over in Tarrytown. Annamarie is an RN in Yonkers. Here, I've made a cup of coffee for you to get you moving. I'm going to go and wake the girls."

Stopping first in the older daughters room, Erin woke Maura. "Get up sleepy head; you know what today is, don't you? Dad is already up, and Molly's little friend will be waiting for us at about 6:30. The weather looks pretty good for late November, and it shouldn't take us too long to get down to the Feis. Dad filed up the gas tank last night, so as soon as you are ready we'll have breakfast and then stop by the Rossi's house to pick them up. I've got to go wake Molly, so get a move on!"

Molly, age 10, was a little bit harder to awaken. But once she was awake her excitement at competing in the year's premier dancing competition, representing Jonnie MacEvoy's Tri-State Academy of Irish Dance, raised her energy level considerably. "We've got to go, mommy, we've got to go! It's late!"

"Hey, Molly, it's not yet 5 AM. Give us a break here, would you?"

By 5:30, showered, combed and with teeth brushed, they were all assembled for breakfast, and by 6:15 were on their way across town to the Rossi's home. The Rossi's daughter Angela met them at the door. "My mom and dad are ready to go, and so am I," she reported. " Hi Maura, Hi Molly!" She shouted as she waved to the girls still sitting in the back of the SUV. "Mom, Dad, let's go let's go, the Lincolns are already here!" In short order, everyone was arranged in the late-model SUV with the girls in the back seats and parents in the front and middle of the vehicle. After a coffee stop at Dunkin' Donuts, they made their way across town to the Garden State Parkway, and then south to the New Jersey Turnpike.

"Where exactly are we going, Pat?" Don asked. Isn't this somewhere in Montgomery County outside Philadelphia?"

"Yes, it is, Don, Pat replied. "It's about 25 miles northwest of Philly. The competition is taking place at the King of Prussia Mall. The organizers have rented the disused J.C. Penny's store for the occasion. The nice thing about that is that if you become bored with the dancing competition, there are lots of places for you to go shopping until we're ready to come back! "

" I know it well, Pat," Don replied. "Annamarie and I both grew up in Philly. Annamarie graduated from Hallahan, and I went to St. Joe's Prep, although we didn't meet until both of us were working in the City." They continued to chat in the front seat of the car, discussing the odds of the New York Giants ever appearing in a Super Bowl again, while Erin and Annamarie talked in the second row. The kids dozed together on the large back row.

"So, tell me at all about this Irish dancing thing," Annamarie said. "Ever since our Angela saw your girls and some of their friends dancing at St. Margaret's on St. Patrick's Day, she's been crazy to learn more about Irish dancing. Which is kind of funny in a way; I am Polish, and Don's family are all Italian. Are they even going to let us in to see the competition, Erin?"

Erin just laughed. "Well, to tell the truth, they'd probably let you in if you were Martians. Generally, most of the people you'll meet at these competitions are either family of the competitors, musicians who have been hired to provide the accompaniment or officials of the dancing schools that are represented in that particular session."

"So why is this competition so critical?" Angela asked. "That's all that Maura and Molly have talked about for the last month or so. Something about qualifying for a special competition if they do well here? Is it some sort of championship, or what?"

Erin laughed again. "Well, the trip to King of Prussia is only going to take about two hours, and I'm not so sure I can explain this quickly, so that it makes any sense. But I'll try. But tell me this, Annamarie, Have you ever heard your parents or grandparents use Polish words to describe things? How about you, Don? Any Italian phrases running around in your mind?"

Both laughed. "Well, my granddad always said 'Jak się masz?' whenever we first came through the door to visit. I think it means something like "How ya doin? Kiddo?"

"Ha! You think that's something?" Don interjected. "You should hear all the old 'Mustache Petes' on the corner of Second and Mifflin, where I grew up. 'Yo Donnie! Buongiorno! Come stai?' Which is Italian for 'Jak się masz' !"

Erin smiled and continued. "Well, I'm as Irish as Paddy's pig, truth to tell. My maiden name was Quinlan, and my mother's maiden name was Leary. And Pat is even more Irish than I am; I'm third generation Irish-American, and his parents were born in Ireland. So when we hear Irish words or phrases, it's second nature for us even if we don't speak the language as well as we should. You'll hear certain phrases bandied around today I'm sure, but here's what some of them mean:

"A *Feis* (plural feiseanna) was originally an opportunity for storytellers to reach a large audience, and often warriors would recount their exploits in combat, clansmen would trace family genealogies, and bards and balladeers would lead the groups in legends, stories, and song. These gatherings eventually gave rise to athletic and sporting competitions, and ultimately a venue for Irish dancing. At this level, dancers can design or choose a costume of their own. Maura's dress features Unicorns; Molly's has sequined dragonflies. Girls usually wear ornate dresses with long sleeves and short skirt and usually wear their hair curled, in a wig, in a bun wig or just down. The cargo area behind the back seat is packed with dresses, wigs, and what-not, and my 'mommy kit' has needles, thread, a first aid kit, and maybe a kitchen sink thrown in for good measure. Pat says I'm like the Coast Guard: 'Semper Paratus – Always Prepared.' And what's this other word, something about octopuses?" Annamarie asked quizzically. Erin laughed again. "That's an *Oireachtas* (plural: Oireachtais): You see, 'back in the day' folks danced at Irish social gatherings just as they did elsewhere in Europe. When you live in a village in the back of beyond, those special dances at the crossroads or the church hall were something to look forward to, I bet! Along about 1730 or so, 'Traveling Dance Masters' appeared on the scene in Ireland and made a major contribution to dancing as we know it today. These were professionals who taught dancing for a living and introduced 'step dancing' -- so-called because it was executed in eight-bar 'steps'. They also introduced a high degree of discipline including the holding of the hands by the side. I know that people think it looks silly, but it's a significant part of our Irish history. It's just like Gaelic football or hurling or even camogie, which our kids play on weekends sometimes. It's something we cherish, because it's, well, a part of who we are."

"Now, the Gaelic League was established in the late nineteenth century to promote all aspects of Irish culture, including Irish Dancing. Fairly soon after, they became the regulating authority for all of these cultural artifacts that help differentiate the Irish from the English. The League introduced dancing classes not only throughout Ireland but everywhere among the Irish diaspora. Irish dancing is now taught all over the world and performed by people with little or no Irish connection but who have been attracted to the dancing because of the intricacies and extreme discipline that the dance requires. Lately, interest in Irish Dance is flourishing; not only here, but in the United Kingdom, Australia and New Zealand and wherever we Irish washed up. I've heard that more than a quarter-million people regularly attend lessons in Irish Dancing, whether step dancing (performed by individuals) or team dancing.""So, given the natural human tendency to organize things, in modern competitive Irish dance, an Oireachtas refers to an annual championship competition. Oireachtas are often held by worldwide Irish dance organizations. The Irish word Oireachtas has come to refer to major top-level competitions, and, yes, it is often casually translated as 'championship'. You see, there are three rounds in

Oireachtas solo competitions. There is a light shoe round, a hard shoe round, and a recall round. For the light shoe round, girls' competitions may require either a reel or a slip jig depending on the age group. In case of a slip jig, only 40 bars are danced. The possible dances for the hard shoe round for girls' competitions are treble jig and hornpipe. You'll see many elements of these dances today when we finally get to King of Prussia. And, finally, the required hard shoe dance for each year is determined by age group. For girls, reel and hornpipe coincide in any given year, and hence slip jig, and treble jig coincide. For treble jig, the dancer is required to perform 48 bars; for hornpipe, the standard is also 40 bars."

"Wow. so, tell me, what makes today's competion so critical?" Annamarie asked. "In North America, Oireachtais are qualifying events for the World Championships. But this year, for the very first time, there will be a "Super-Oireachtas" held in Cape Breton, Nova Scotia, the only Gaelic speaking region in North America. Don't tell the girls, though, but it's *Scots Gaelic* first brought to Canada by displaced Highlanders over 250 years ago. That's why today's competition is so important. Maura was quite close last year; generally, the top two competitors in each age group are selected to go forward, and Maura was third. Molly is coming along strong, however, and if both of them made it to the next level, well quite frankly I'd be over the moon. Irish dance has been part of my own life since I was their age; in fact, I nearly made it to the highest levels back when I was an active dancer. But most of all, it was fun; I don't want this to sound like it's drudgery or anything like that. We always tell our girls, just as my mom told me, 'the time to stop is when it's not fun anymore.' And if you and Angela get involved in Irish dance, I bet you'll feel the same way. " They continued chatting among themselves, as the three girls dozed in the rear seat. They crossed into Pennsylvania at the Turnpike entrance and proceeded to the major interchange at Valley Forge. And, from there, it was a short jog down Allenwood road till they reached the dance venue shortly before 9:00 AM.

IRISH DANCERS IN CHINA

DANCE DANCE WHEREVER YOU MIGHT BE

IRISH DANCING IN PERTH, WESTERN AUSTRALIA

IRISH DANCING IN AUKLAND NEW ZEALAND

IRISH DANCING IN CAPETOWN

CHAPTER TWO: BE PROUD OF OUR COUNTRY AND GOOD OLD C.B.

While the Lincoln and Rossi families were traveling toward the Midwest Regional Feis at King of Prussia, Pennsylvania, the ad hoc working group planning the Grand Oireachtas in Nova Scotia met at the boardroom of Cape Breton University.

The commission, established by the provincial legislature two years earlier in celebration of the four hundredth anniversary of the affiliation of Cape Breton Island with Nova Scotia, represented all the stakeholders vital to the success of the Oireachtas. Chaired by the Honourable Sandra Miller, a former member of the provincial Legislative Assembly, it represented all levels of government. Each organization had several representatives and alternates, and a full plenary session often consisted of thirty-five participants or more.

Ms. Miller called the meeting to order. "It's good to see you all again. Just looking at the sign-in sheets leads me to believe that every component organization has at least one representative present. That should help us to move things along smoothly."

To give some additional structure to our discussions, I'd like to address issues step-by-step; starting with the arrival and housing of the participants. With that thought in mind, I'll first call upon Adam Fortin of the Federal Department of Immigration, Refugees, and Citizens for an update, please."

Inspector Fortin arose to speak. "Since our last meeting, I have been in contact with our office in Ottawa and informed them of the issues which have surfaced at our previous meetings. They have agreed that they will allow temporary visitor visas for anyone arriving at Sydney Airport (YQY), who is bearing a letter or other documents indicating that they are participants or family members of participants in the Oireachtas. For those arriving by automobile, we will also notify the IRC representatives at each boarding crossing point in Ontario, Quebec, New Brunswick, and Nova Scotia to accept the same documents. I also suggest that those with a closer relationship with the Irish-dancing associations strongly urge their participants and families to take advantage of the special charter flights which are being organized. Given our heightened security, it's a lot easier to pre-certify travelers at Boston Logan than here. You *are* using Logan, right?" he asked, turning to Ms. Anna Brennan, the senior Oireachtas coordinator.

That's correct, Inspector," she replied, "and I will discuss the charter flights when Madam Chairperson indicates that it's our turn."

Other than that, there's not much else to add," he

concluded. "The timing on this event is quite fortunate, since earlier in July we expect there will be a surge in tourism because of the other 400-year celebrations activities planned throughout the province, but later in the month things should slow down. After all, in the scope of tourism through Atlantic Canada, a thousand or so additional visitors is not a very large issue at all."

"Thanks, Inspector" replied Ms. Miller, and "I'm certain that your team will ensure a delightful welcome to these visitors to Canada, many of whom I suspect have never visited Nova Scotia before."

"The next issue, of course, is housing. Jordan King, representing Destination Canada, what can you add to this discussion?"

Mr. Jordan King, of 'Destination Canada,' rose to speak. "I believe I have excellent news indeed. We have explored leasing an appropriate vessel for ten days starting July 21, and have tentatively identified MV TORSHAVN, of the Faeroe Islands Shipping Corporation. This vessel will complete a repositioning cruise from northern Europe en route to Boston, from which it will sail in coastal waters, both here and in the States. The fixed rate for a bare-ship rental is US $250,000 for the ten-day period. It has been suggested that since there are accommodations for 1200 passengers on the ship, we could establish a daily rate of about $100 US per person per day and offset the cost of the bare-ship lease. All service staff and the essential engineering staff, mainly Scandinavian, would remain on board while the ship is in Sydney. Captain of the Sydney port, Captain McGregor, can provide additional details."

Captain Jock McGregor took the floor "As you all know, summertime is usually busy at our cruise pier in Sydney. Fortunately, however, we have no cruise vessels calling during these weeks. And there are no technical reasons why we could not easily accommodate MV TORSHAVN. She is one of the smaller cruise vessels which we could accommodate in proximity to the Joan Harriss Pavilion downtown. The dock has a draft of 16.5 meters and the published specifications for TORSHAVN indicating maximum draft of 13.9 meters when fully loaded. I have reviewed the three most recent safety inspection reports for the vessel, and aside from minor habitability issues, it is acceptable in all respects. I am not qualified to speak to the issue of the financial viability of the proposal under discussion, but the seaworthiness of this vessel is not in question. We have also discussed the matter with the management of the Joan Harriss Pavilion, and with your permission, I will turn the floor over to Susan Jackson, the director."

The chairperson politely interrupted, however. "Before you stand down Capt. McGreggor I have one or two questions concerning the security of this vessel, or of any similar vessel when it's in the Port of Sydney. Can you describe the security provisions which you normally employ in this type of situation?"

"Certainly," he replied. "Transport Canada's marine security programs assist in protecting Canada's marine transportation system against unlawful interference, terrorist attacks or use as a means to attack our allies. In particular, The Marine Security Enforcement Team (MSET) program is a joint RCMP-Canadian Coast Guard (CCG) project that enhances marine security throughout Atlantic Canada. The program combines the law enforcement powers of the RCMP with CCG vessels and expertise to provide an armed, on-water law enforcement capacity throughout Atlantic Canada."

RCMP Inspector Owen Pelletier then rose to speak. "With your permission Madam Chairperson, I will defer this entire issue of security for our visitors until the end of our discussions of logistics. I am also sure that Staff Sgt. Marie Morrison representing the Cape Breton Regional Police Service (CBRP)will also be able to shed additional light on that critical topic."

"Very well," replied the chairperson, "So with that, let me call once again call upon Susan Jackson of the Joan Harriss Pavilion for whatever additional information she may have, especially concerning transportation for our visitors directly from the ship to the dance completion at Cape Breton University."

" I'm sure most of you are familiar with the Pavilion and the facilities we have available. We'll make them available to the committee to use as required. We have several meeting rooms and public spaces which we can dedicate to this exceptional event, especially Pittman Hall which seats 800 people banquet-style or 1200 people for concerts. We can also divide Pittman Hall into two smaller spaces, seating 300 people banquet-style or 500 people for concerts. Personally, I feel that by working closely with the ship's officers when they arrive and coordinating with the Cape Breton-Victoria Regional School Board Representatives we will be able to coordinate the loading and discharging of the dancers and their families from dockside to the University. I know that their transportation coordinator, Jim Breslin will go into further detail as to how these guests will be transported out to Cape Breton University."

Jim Breslin rose and commented, "We have sixty vehicles available for transportation. Most are capable of seating forty students comfortably, although the adults in the party may find them a bit cramped. Eight other vehicles are smaller, accommodating twenty-four students, (we call them our 'Jeeps'); They are the vehicles you may see serving smaller communities here on the island. We propose to work in rotation, with the first vehicles departing approximately one hour before their scheduled arrival time at the University. That should allow sufficient time for orderly loading and transport of the participants. We're quite fortunate that the route we have chosen between Esplanade Street downtown and the University is straightforward. Buses will stage on Charlotte Street and load in front of the Pavilion, and then depart up Dorchester Street, and then along Grand Lake Rd. to CBU and unload wherever directed by the University staff. I estimate that under normal traffic conditions this trip of slightly less than 12 km will take fewer than 15 minutes. None of the routes selected are subject to very heavy traffic even during rush hour, and I would estimate that the maximum time required will be no more than 20 minutes in each direction. We've arranged with the Pavilion staff to hold the "Jeeps" in reserve in the case of late arrivals or stragglers. We have asked our regular staff of experienced drivers to be available for this special event, and in fact, they will be on the payroll on the first day of the event and remain so, since school will be starting again shortly after the completion of this dance competition. All in all, we look forward to serving you on this significant event in the history of Cape Breton and Nova Scotia. Now, what questions might you have?"

There were no questions, and the chairperson then called upon the representative of Cape Breton University, Assistant Dean for Outreach, Doctor Olivia Adams.

"Well without denigrating my home province of PEI, I can't recall a time when everyone came together with such a clear focus, and single purpose in mind. This province's unofficial motto "'Céad Míle Fáilte' certainly applies in this instance."

"That said, I have some information which may be useful to you. I recently received from the 'Grand Oireachtas' team, the specifications for the stages required for the Oireachtas and I have shared those with our facilities department. They tell us that, with one or two minor exceptions, these temporary stages should present no problem. Let me read to you some of the specifications which the forwarded to my office:

Dance Stage Specifications

The following specifications must be used to provide consistent dance stages among the various Oireachtas:

I. Stage Materials: Unless the dance floor stages used are a permanent part of the venue where the dance competitions are performed, the dance stages may be plywood or other similar material. Composition/particle board does not stand up under hard shoe dancing and, if damaged, cannot be repaired. Therefore, it is not recommended as a dancing surface.

No substance that can become airborne can be used on a stage/dance floor in an attempt to improve traction.

For the safety of dancers, we no longer allow Oireachtas to place dance floors or other rolled out types of flooring materials directly on cement or concrete floors for all grades and championships at all Oireachtas.

Championship Stages: Stages should be at least 20' deep x 24' wide for championship dancing.

"As I said, our facilities folks have no problem meeting these specifications. Our planning engineer has told me that they intend to construct the temporary stages using 3cm sheets of plywood as suggested in the memo. He also has made preliminary measurements and intends to use 12 foot, 2X6 joints, on 40cm centers to better support the platforms and has even added several metal hand grips to facilitate moving the stages pieces from place to place."

"Additionally with the help of the facilities engineering group we have identified four venues on the campus where we can establish the stages and still provide sufficient seating for family and friends. These four venues are:

The Boardmore Playhouse-one stage; the RBC Theatre-one stage; the Canada Games Complex-four stages, (using the space made available from the recent decommissioning of the hockey rink,) and lastly the Soccer Dome-four stages. The total number of seats for spectators, family, and friends is no fewer than 213 in each of the venues, with Broadmore Playhouse and the RBC Theatre having 500 or more seats available. In conversations with the Nova Scotia Grand Oireachtas team, they tell me that this will be more than sufficient to meet their needs. And while the walking distances on our campus are not large, we can assist in the rapid unloading of the dancers and their families by providing a daily list of the specific stage upon which each will dance. If our friends at the Harriss Center are amenable, and the committee gives us daily updates, we can either email or fax the list of stage assignments directly to the Harriss Center and also give copies to each of the bus drivers. Campus security will set up dedicated routes among the venues on the campus so that the dancers can be delivered directly to the closest point of approach to the stage upon which they will be dancing that day."

"Finally, in keeping with what I understand is good practice at these Oireachtas, we are pleased to be able to make available separate housing arrangements for adjudicators, staff and visiting media. We have three options available: 125 rooms at Alumni Hall; an additional 125 rooms available at Cabot Residence; and finally 110 rooms at Harris Hall. So we believe that we have enough space for any of the officials of the Oireachtas, as we've been informed that it is good practice to separate the officials of the championship from the competitors. I'm happy to answer whatever questions you may have now."

Constable Cameron McDonald of the Cape Breton Regional Police raised his hand.

"I do think that I have an issue which has not been submitted for consideration. That concerns the health and safety of the participants as well as those who accompany them. We have nine hospitals here on Cape Breton, but there are only two which in my estimation are equipped to handle the visitors, or in the worst case, a mass casualty event. Those are of course Cape Breton Regional Hospital, and to a lesser extent, Glace Bay General, which although more limited does have the advantage of being closer to the University. Has anyone taken into consideration the needs for emergency or even routine medical care during this event?"

It was clear from the reaction of the committee members that this had yet to be addressed. The chairperson responded. "I will take that issue as my own, and contact the administrators of both healthcare facilities and seek their input. I would not be surprised to see representatives of either or both of those hospitals at our next planning meeting."

"We come now to the final agenda item; public safety during the Oireachtas," the chairperson announced. As we all know, multiple public safety agencies operate in the Province of Nova Scotia, and two, in particular, have responsibilities here on Cape Breton. I call upon RCMP Inspector Owen Pelletier and Staff Sgt Marie Morrison of the Cape Breton Regional Police to enlighten us on these issues."Inspector Pelletier and Staff Sgt. Morrison rose and walked to the podium. Inspector Pelletier spoke first. "As I promised at our previous meeting, I have been in contact with RCMP's provincial command and have submitted our plan a for this regional event. As someone mentioned earlier, one thousand additional visitors is not a particularly large increase over our normal summer surge of visitors, but there are one or two additional issues which are quite important. The first is that we live in dangerous times, even here on Cape Breton, which we tend to think of as an island far away from the worries of the world. Would that it be so! I do think that the challenges here on Cape Breton are different from those in Toronto, Montreal or even Halifax, but there are challenges none the less. The first of those is the task of keeping hundreds of young women safe while they are coming and going from the University campus. And the second impact has to do with automotive traffic. Moving sixty or more school buses on the same route within a limited amount of time presents its unique challenges. Without disclosing plans which are best kept confidential, I can assure you that provincial command of the RCMP is well aware of the potential dangers that can occur here. We will have additional staff brought in from other areas of the province, and if necessary from outside the province to ensure the safety of everyone concerned. As to the traffic issues, let me turn to our good colleague Staff Sgt. Marie Morrison, whose organization is charged with automotive safety here in the province. Marie?"Staff Sgt. Morrison approached the microphone. "As every good police department does, we believe that prevention is much better than reaction. In that spirit, we plan to step up inspection of the school buses used in shuttling participants and their families to and from downtown to the University campus. That inspection will be completed well before the first participants arrive here on the island. The second issue is traffic enforcement. We will have additional constables strategically stationed along the approximately twelve km route between the piers and the University campus. We've also had some discussions with the security department at the University. We have offered, and the security chief at the University has accepted our assistance in ensuring that those routes are not only efficient but are also safe for the participants. As an example, we have suggested routes that do not include left turns, as well as routes which do not involve a Yield-Sign equipped intersection. We will also have at least one constable on the campus throughout the entire Oireachtas. There are other elements of the security plan which I am not authorized to disclose publicly, and I am sure that the inspector's position is the same. But believe me when I say, as the mother of three young daughters myself, that keeping these kids safe is of the utmost importance to me, and I am certain to every constable in the Northeast District."

 The chairperson intervened. "Thank you both for your understanding and for your cooperation in making this a safe and pleasant environment for all of our visitors. And with that, the hour grows late and I think we have completed our agenda for the day. But first, this announcement – thanks to a generous offer from our friends at the Harriss Pavilion, we now have a conference room available to us for our bi-monthly meetings. With the winter weather closing in quickly upon us I'm sure that those of you who are residents of Sydney appreciate not having to drive out to the University campus. And so our next meeting will be two weeks from Saturday, and we will meet in the conference room at the Harriss Center."

CHAPTER THREE: I DANCED IN THE MORNING

Both the parents and the girls raced from the car to line up at the registration desk. They had been able to pre-register online, but they needed to pick up their dancing Competitor Number Card at the registration desk as well as to find out on which of the eight identical stages each would dance. While the Rossi family were distracted, Pat Lincoln paid $15.00 into the registrars to cover the "Family Fee" for their visitors. "No sense in causing them any embarrassment," Pat thought to himself. "Our kids certainly enjoy having a classmate with them to share the dancing experience today."

The girls checked their cards, and Maura exclaimed, "Mom, we're in luck today! Both of our cards end in 7! See, my card is 1417 and Molly's is 1237"! Both sets of parents laughed. They received their schedules and were dancing almost concurrently, but on stages widely separated on the now disused JC Penny main sales floor.

As was the usual case, the girls were separated both by the specific stages where would perform and the times that they needed to report to the stage monitor. "It happens so often that we don't ever expect that both of us will see the same kid performing at the same time," Erin commented to Annamarie. "And that's not unusual, given the wide range of age-groups; there are many more dancers in Maura's age group than Molly's. But I've got a suggestion; why don't you guys, Pat and Don, wander around and take in the scenery while Annamarie and I go with the girls to the dressing room. And if you two guys happen to find some reasonably tasting coffee anywhere in this mausoleum, you will bring some back for us, right?"

Both dads nodded, and making their way through the growing crowds entering the ad hoc dance arena, wandered around observing some of the other vendors who were setting up their booths along the walls of the venue. An Oireachtas was an All-Irish Festival; vendors were selling baked goods (with soda bread prominently displayed), while other vendors sold CDs of Irish and other Celtic music, and there were even a few selling musical instruments.

"Hmm," Pat said to Don, "I've always wanted to own a Bodhran." "A moron," exclaimed Don, "you oughta come to work with me someday. We have lots of them in my building."

"We have a few ourselves," replied Pat. "But it's not a *Moron*, it's a *Bodhran*, which is a sort of Irish goatskin drum. You'll probably see some of the musicians playing them today, and, just like the drummers we had in our pickup bands when I was a kid, most of them get the job because they couldn't play anything else! But it's not as easy as it looks; you hold the Bodhran in one hand and play it with a two-headed stick, called a tipper, held in the other hand, and you can change the tone of the instrument by how you hold the crossbars in the back. I briefly had one when I was a kid, but my kid brothers, John and Dennis broke the skin when they were kidding around. Sure wish I had another one, though!"

"Say, Pat, I noticed a *Coming Soon* sign when we came to the mall property. Any idea what's happening here?"

"Well," Pat said, "You know I'm in the commercial real estate business in New York City. I haven't heard much about it, but I understand the property developers here are concerned about retail sales declining because of internet growth. This mall seems to be about an 80,000-foot space, hard to fill in today's market. I doubt there are many large retailers in the market for "anchor space" these days. Large malls such as King of Prussia are going to have to scramble, or they're going to find themselves going out of business. It's happened to a fair number of shopping mall developers already, and it's perhaps the least attractive segment of commercial real estate today."

"But here's an idea. The rest of the mall is opening now, and I bet you there are some excellent coffee shops not far from this end of the mall. Let's wander out among the "real people" and see if we can find some coffee for ourselves and our wives. I think they would appreciate something from Starbucks or even a good Dunkin'

Donuts, and we won't have to go out to one of the outlying buildings here on the mall property.

They were in luck. Not twenty yards from the connecting entrance into the mall, they found an open Starbucks. Both men knew exactly what their spouses would most enjoy and both ordered coffee for themselves and their wives and returned to the ad-hoc dancing arena.

As the dutiful dads and were wandering the gigantic mall, Erin and Annamarie and the three girls rushed back out to their car and brought in the various pieces of the dancing costumes for both Maura and Molly.

"Where do you get the dresses?" Annamarie asked. "They must cost a fortune!"

"Well, they do, and they don't! If we were to buy these directly from Ireland, and several companies there specialize in Irish dance costumes now, they would cost an arm and a leg. But realizing that preteen and teenage girls outgrow anything you buy them even before the price tag is removed, a very good mom-to-mom underground has grown over the last 20 years or so. Most Feis and Oireachtas moms scan the bulletin boards and forums for dresses in their daughter's size or, if they're particularly clever, in their next size. Often you can even swap an existing dress for a larger dress if the other mom has more than one daughter dancing. That's what I do. The downside is, of course, you get what you get and not necessarily what your daughter might want. But we explained to Maura and Molly that as much as we love Irish dance, we're not made of money. And they grow to like the dancing costume which they were wearing at any given time. One unexpected benefit is that when we take photographs, particularly if they have done well in the competition, we can always look at the dress and say, 'Oh, that was in Pittsburgh, or maybe in New Orleans!' So it all works out."

They returned to the venue and made their way to the dressing area. It sounded like mass chaos inside as they entered, and perhaps it was. At least 100 young girls and women aged eight to over twenty were milling about with mothers or best friends in attendance preparing for the dance competition, now just an hour or so away. Some of the youngest girls seemed to be near to tears, but at the end, everyone's costume was correctly adjusted, her dancing wig (if worn) was held accurately with inconspicuous bobby pins, and the smell of tanning spray was pungent in the air.

"So, tell me: How do they set up the levels of competition?" Annamarie asked.

"Well, the dancers 'Feis Age' is her age as of January 1st of the current year. For example – Molly was eleven years old on January 1, so she's in the U-12 division. Maura is nearly fifteen but her birthday was after January First, so she's still in the U-14 group. And they are further divided by proficiency: there are six grades: Beginner, Advanced Beginner, Novice, Advanced, Preliminary Championship winners and Open Championship winners. Maura ranks as Advanced and Molly is a Novice, but she's coming along fast!"

"And what about makeup?" Annamarie continued.

"Good question. Make-up is verboten for dancers up to and including the U12 age group in the beginning grades (Beginner, Advanced Beginner). Nails must not have colored nail polish. Jewelry, including necklaces and dangling earrings, must also not be worn."

"And, before you ask, the most controversial question in the last ten years or so has been about the use of "spray tan" on the dancers, particularly the youngest ones. At first I was 100% against it; after all these girls are predominantly Irish Americans, and much of the dancing season is in the winter or early spring, so why should they look like they just came back from Myrtle Beach or somewhere. For a while, moms were about equally divided on the issue, but in the end, the "sprays" prevailed, and now most moms feel compelled to use it in competitions, particularly in competitions such as this when so much is at stake. It's just another facet of preparation I suppose."

Meanwhile, Pat and Don returned to the venue and looked around urgently for the dressing area. They finally saw a young woman wearing a volunteer tag and asked her how they could get to the woman's dressing her room. The young lady laughed and pointed to a side alcove where Pat and Don found two disused escalators, one roped off with safety flags, and the other one serving as a staircase to the second level. They trudged up the escalator, and when they finally reached the top, they saw two female Mall security officers guarding a doorway marked MNA. There was another doorway a few feet to their left marked FIR, although with no security guards present. They approached the female security officers and asked if they could deliver the coffee to their wives who were assisting their daughters.

"Not on your life, gentlemen. If you need something delivered one of us can take it in, but if *you* walk in, you're liable to be mobbed by some irate mothers!" They handed her the coffee, and as they waited outside the door could hear her, in her best stentorian voice calling "Coffee for Mrs. Lincoln - Coffee for Mrs. Rossi!"

Pat and Don laughed. " And what is this MNA and FIR I

see on the signs, Pat?"

"Ah, some crucial words to know in the Irish language, Don. FIR is Irish for men, and MNA is Irish for women. If you only learn two Irish words from your day at the Feis, learn these, or you are apt to commit a social error if you are looking for the restrooms, buddy."

They waited off to the side, while the flow of mothers and daughters leaving the dressing room and descending the erstwhile stairs became a torrent. In just a few minutes, they saw the Lincoln and Rossi women passing through the doorway. Pat drew in a long breath. The girls looked stunning; Maura in her unicorn patterned dress and Molly in her dress featuring sequined dragonflies. Maura wore a full hairpiece of red ringlets complementing her red hair, while Molly wore a bun, in appreciation of her smaller stature. Erin suggested they wait until the crowd had thinned out on the escalator. "You wouldn't want to go there just now; there's a real risk of someone tripping and falling and getting trampled at the bottom. I have the schedule here; let's review what we're going to do, and then we can head directly to the appropriate stages when we finally get down on the main floor."

"Maura: You start here on the northeast side of the dance floor, on stage number four. Your schedule indicates that you will start at 9:15 and your last qualifying dance before the Callbacks should be about 11:40 or so. You know that times do slip as we go through the day right?" Maura nodded yes. "Your first two sessions are:

Stage 4 NE Corner Pair 8 Report 9:25 A.M.

Stage 4 NE Corner Pair 8 Report 11:05 A.M.

Molly: You have a bit longer before you have to report to the stage monitor. You start on stage number two on the west side of the dance floor. That's not very far away from the foot of this escalator, so be careful when you get off. And your last scheduled dance is right at noon, so if we go to lunch, we're going to have to be very quick about it. We'll let your dads figure out when and where we should go OK, Molly?" Molly nodded in agreement.

Stage 2 West Side Pair 8 Report 9:50 A.M.

Stage 2 West Side Pair 8 Report 12:05 P.M.

"What tunes are we going to dance to, mom?" Erin continued to review the schedule.

"Maura, you're in luck. You've seen all of these pieces many times in other Feis, the only one that may be unusual is the one selected for the callback for your age group. You have: *The Battle of Arklow, The Silver Spear,* and *High Cauled Cap* for the callback."

Molly: Yours may be a little bit more difficult for you, but

I know you can handle them. You have: *The Garden Of Daisies, The Musical Priest, King of the Fairies,* and *the Eight Handed Jig.* You are in the eighth pair to dance in your age group, so you get to hear the same tunes over and over again. If you make it to the callbacks you will have a familiar one, you know how the *Eight Handed Jig* goes, you danced that at St. Margaret's last St. Patrick's day, didn't you?"

"Okay, guys. Who wants to go where? Don and Pat, do you want to go to watch Maura, while Annamarie, Angela and I go with Molly? We can swap out after the second set, and if we make it to the callbacks, we will all go together." Both dads nodded affirmatively.

"Okay everybody, if you want to chance the escalator it looks like the crowd is thinning out. Be very careful at the bottom. You know how some of these 'country folks,' tended to bunch up on the street or at the bottom of stairs. Personally, I think walking in New York City is taking your life into your own hands, but this may very well be a close second."

They descended the nonworking escalator with no difficulties, and with a quick look around, split into two groups. "See you guys in a little bit," Annamarie shouted over the crowd noise. "And don't forget to find us a place for lunch!"

Pat and Don followed Maura who was, after all, an experienced Feis and Oireachtas participant. "What kind of music is this?" Don asked Pat.

"Well, there are three types in your average step-dancing competition:

Reels: A beginner dance, done in soft shoes to 2/2 or 4/4 time. It is a very athletic dance with lots of jumping around.

Hornpipes: The hornpipe is a hard shoe dance done in 4/4 time with a one-and-two-and-three-and-four count with accents on one and three. There are both fast and slow hornpipes.

Jigs: Jigs are another common type of dance; Like the reel, the tune usually consists of two parts made of eight bars, but the time signature is 6/8, meaning that there are six beats to every bar."

"But you can forget all the counting and beats to the bar, Don.
If you can say 'carrots and cabbages, carrots and cabbages' in time to the music, it's a jig. If you can say 'double-decker, double-decker' in time to the music, it's a reel.

Hornpipes usually go 'Humpty Dumpty, Humpty Dumpty'. But the real give away that it is a hornpipe is that each section ends with three quarter-notes."

" But let's go. The girls are about to start the dancing."

CHAPTER FOUR: I DANCED IN THE EVENING

About a minute after the Lincoln and Rossi clans found their dance stages, a rapid tapping on the microphone at the front of the venue quieted the crowd slightly and indicated an announcement was forthcoming. Máire Maighréad Mac Eafartaigh (nee Mary Margaret McCafferty) a retired postal worker from Buffalo who was the current chairperson of the mid-Atlantic region, called for attention. She then greeted and welcomed all the participants in rusty but serviceable Irish, and then switched to English. She turned the microphone over to Father Patrick O'Hanlon, of Mother Of Divine Providence Parish on Allendale Road who offered a brief benediction, thankfully only in English.

And with that, the Feis began. The musicians, mostly older men, started tuning their instruments. One played the button box accordion, another a fiddle, and yet the third played the Bodran. "You know, Don, I've heard a lot of parents remark that it takes more skill to be a Feis musician that it does to play in a club or with an Irish band. Notice how each musician has a metronome by his side. Parents get very irate if the musicians accompanying their daughter's presentation are even slightly off time. If I ever do get a Bodran, I promise I will not become a Feis musician.

The dancing began, and Maura and all the young ladies

in the U-14 group performed competently and artistically. While Pat watched the dancers though, Don seemed more interested in watching the two very attractive adjudicators. Between the first and second sessions, both husbands regrouped near Molly's stage with their wives. "How did it go here?" Pat asked. "Molly was fantastic," Erin replied. "She nailed it as far as I can see. There were a couple of mishaps though, but none happened when Molly was on stage."

"One poor girl apparently developed vertigo during the very energetic reel and collapsed and passed out right on the stage. Fortunately, her mom and dad were here, and they helped her up and took her out of the venue. There was another dancer a few sets later, who seemed to lose her sense of space, and who danced dangerously near the front of the stage. Fortunately, as you can see, the stage is only about eighteen inches off the floor. But she could've damaged her ankle or something if she danced off into thin air. How was Maura?"

"She did a bang-up job," Pat replied. "Each time I see her dancing, she seems to get better and better. Hey Don, you were watching the judges during Maura's dance, did you get any clues as to what they were writing on their score sheets?"

"Beats me," Don replied, laughing. " I was sitting at an angle and couldn't see what they were writing. All I could see were the tent cards saying where they were from. One, I noticed, was from the Hoosier School of Irish dance in Indianapolis, and the other was from the Buckeye Academy of Irish Arts, in Columbus Ohio. But as to what they were writing on the score sheets; no I couldn't see any of that."

"One judge is from Columbus Ohio?" asked Molly. "Maybe she knows our Uncle John!" She was referring, of course, to the world-renowned author, whose many books on military topics continue to be read and quoted around the world.

"No, Molly, I really don't think they run in the same circles," her mom ruefully replied.

"You know, Don, back when I was a senior dancer I got involved in judging some small informal groups at the Dancing Academy I attended. Let me see if I can remember some of the critical points on the standard scoring sheet." She thought for a moment.

"Well, if I remember correctly they included such things as *Arm And Hand Positions, Strong, Clear Taps* for hard shoe dances, Elevation on leaps and, very importantly a cheerful facial expression. *Flexibility, Posture,* and *Timing* also play a part.

I do remember one of my own teachers who was an experienced adjudicator remind us all that one of the things she liked to see was the ability to "hide your mistakes," By that I mean that if you happen to get off the beat with the music, just toss in some extra steps until you get back to where you should be. And if you make a mistake, whatever you do, don't stop dancing!"

Most of the adjudicators are looking for the totality of the dance more than anything else, and while they might make a mental note of an area where you failed in one of these characteristics, nevertheless they might not deduct points from your total score. And I've often thought that the first impression you make when you come onto the stage helps sets the tone for the adjudicator and how he or she sees you in the context of all of the other dancers that day. But that's just my opinion."

"So how is the scoring system set up?" Don asked.

"Well, competitions for each dance are scored on a 100-point system, which reflects the subjective opinion of each different judge. Most scores seem to be in the 50-90 point range and can vary wildly depending upon the adjudicator. For Individual dance competitions, placing is based entirely on a single judge's subjective opinion."

Just then a five-minute warning sounded, announcing the imminent start of the second round. "Before you guys go, do you want to trade places?"

"Sure," Pat replied, "Is that okay with you, Don?"

"If you don't mind, I may have a better idea," said Don. "We were discussing what to do about lunch, and it looks like we're running a bit late in the program already, so I propose to leave midway during the second session and order lunch for everyone and grab a table. Lunch is on us, by the way. I noticed a Tony's Sandwich Shop in the food court of the mall. I've been told they have pretty good steak sandwiches there. Would any of you like a Philly steak sandwich for lunch?"

All of the adults readily agreed. The girls, however, were concerned about spoiling their dance costumes and asked for something different. Don pulled a Tony's menu from his pocket, and all three girls chose salads. "I knew you guys would like the idea of a fast lunch. That way we could take a break before coming back for the third session and still avoid the heavy crowds which are going to descend upon that food court as soon as the second session ends."

"Mom, we had better get a move on. I don't want to miss the second session," Maura said forcefully. "Come on!"

Erin rolled her eyes but tapped Annamarie on the shoulder. "When you gotta go, you gotta go! See you guys after this session!"

All arrived where they needed to be in good order. The second session went well; both Molly and Maura where outstanding, and both sets of parents, as well as little Angela, were suitably impressed. After Molly had completed her dance, Don left the main venue and walked quickly to Tony's Sandwich Shop in the mall's food court. He placed his order and while waiting for it to be completed grabbed a table close to the wall. He soon covered the table with four wax-paper covered steak sandwiches (with peppers and onions on the side in a little plastic bags), and a couple of minutes later Erin, Pat, Annamarie and the girls arrived out of breath at the food court. By the time the last dancer finished, the food court was packed. "Half the families are going out of the mall, and I think the other half is just about a minute behind us."

"How did Molly do, Pat?"

"She was fantastic. I know that I overuse that word a lot, but I can't think of a better word to describe it. I'm not as up-to-date on judging standards as you are, Erin, but I do know how to read faces fairly well, and the judges seemed very happy as they were scoring her dance. Her dance partner for this session was not as great. Even I could tell that she was having trouble following the music. How did Molly do?"

"Very very well," replied Erin. "Both she and the girl dancing with her did well in my opinion, but from where we were sitting we couldn't see the adjudicators well either. But by the time we finish lunch here they should have the scores posted on a bulletin board near the dressing area and we can see what happens next. But I'm very proud of both of you girls. Honestly, I am. Now let's dig in and finish lunch and then we can go see how you've done."

They finished lunch quickly, and return to the corridor adjacent to the dressing area. The scores for the first two rounds had just been posted. Erin braved the crowd surrounding the bulletin board and returned breathlessly. "Both of you girls are through to the callback around! Maura, you scored 91 and Molly you scored 89. I am so proud of you!"

"Let's make one more stop if we can, " Erin asked. It's time for all of us ladies to visit the 'MNA.' The callback round will be on the main stage, and only the top twelve competitors in each age group made it to the callback. OK ladies, let's leave this crowd and joined the line going to that other important room!

As they returned to the main floor of the venue, they heard an announcement. "Will the top twelve age group participants in the first and second session please return to the main stage area immediately. We're about to begin the callbacks for all age groups."

The Lincoln and Rossi families returned quickly to the

main stage, which was elevated six feet higher than the smaller stages used in the first and second rounds. The chairperson stepped to the microphone and announced. "This callback session may be different from any you have experienced before. There are two reasons for that. Firstly, we have use of this facility only until 6 PM this evening; secondly, we've been monitoring the weather forecasts, and there is substantial snow predicted for later this evening. I know that many of you have come from great distances, and we want you to be safely out of here well before the snowstorm. So if you would listen carefully I'm going to describe how we've modified the call back procedure."

"Each age group will dance separately. Each age group will dance twice, once to the familiar tune listed on your schedule and secondly to an age-appropriate tune listed for each age group. These two tunes will be separated by a three-minute interval. Dancers will perform in groups of four, repeat four, because of the time constraints. There will be a panel of four adjudicators; two from Hoosier School of Irish Dance in Indianapolis, and two from the Buckeye Academy of Irish Arts, of Columbus. During the first dance each adjudicator will focus on one dancer, and after the short interval, they will observe and evaluate another dancer. At the conclusion of each age group, the adjudicators will confer and decide rankings of the participants."

"The names of only the top four participants in each age group will be announced; all others will be listed as semi-finalists. Of the four highest-rated dancers in each age group, the top two will go forward to the North American Oireachtas in late July at Cape Breton University, Nova Scotia. Additional information will be provided to those participants, and the third and fourth finisher will be listed as alternates in case either of the two top finalists is unable to continue to Nova Scotia."

" We'll now begin with the U-10 group. The other finalists should remain near this stage to move things along as quickly as possible."

Both families watched with interest as the U-10 age group took the stage and performed their assigned numbers. "They're pretty darn good for little kids," Molly remarked.

"Little kids," Maura replied. "Look who's talking!"

'Shush you two, Erin said sternly. "You know what this means to these kids. It means the same as it does to you, so be quiet and let them dance!"

Because the U-10 age group was the smallest in the Feis, their competition was soon completed and the four adjudicators conferred at the judging table. It's fair to say that the parents of the U-10s were undoubtedly the most anxious in the room. But Máire Maighréad Mac

Eafartaigh soon returned to the stage and called the U-12 group to attention. "Since there are twelve finalists in your age group, as well as twelve in the U-14s, we will continue to dance in groups of four with the judging precisely as I have outlined earlier." Please come forward, and the monitors will assign you to each dancing group. This they did, and Molly was in the first group, and she and her three fellow dancers took the stage.

The Lincolns and Rossi's were fortunate to have seats with a very good view of the dancers. Molly was second from the left, and her smile was radiant and visible not only to her parents in the audience but also to the adjudicators at the judging table. When the dancing began, it was clear that Molly had listened carefully to her dance teachers and also to her mom. Her excellent presentation and skill were evident to everyone watching. Don Rossi continued to try to gauge the reaction of the adjudicators, but the angle of view from the seating area to the judging table was acute. At the short three-minute interval, most of the dancers stopped to catch their breath, but Molly, with a fixed smile in place, stood quietly waiting for the second number to begin. And begin it did! Molly danced as if she were in tryouts for a road show of Riverdance, and Erin just whispered to herself, "Come on Molly: you're doing well, perfect PERFECT!" At the completion of the U-12 age group, as the adjudicators conferred, Molly came down to join her family. "You could never have done better than that, Molly. I m so so proud of you!" her mother remarked.

"U-14 dancers to the stage please! Again there were twelve dancers and the monitor assigned positions in the dance. This time, Maura was in the last section dancing and was at the far right side of the line of four dancers. And once again, although there was a certain understandable family bias in favor of the Lincoln girls, all knew her presentation was excellent. Even when the dancer to her immediate left missed several steps and was struggling to recover, Maura kept dancing as if there were no tomorrow. Just like Molly, Maura was a real trooper and stood taking shallow breaths until the dancing started again. Her second presentation was as flawless as the first, and when she returned to her family, her parents were equally proud of the beautiful exhibition she had just performed.

The dancing continued through all of the age groups. Finally, at the completion of the U-20 group, Ms. Mac Eafartaigh thanked the adjudicators and wished them a safe journey home to the Midwest Region and announce a short interval until all of the scores were tabulated.

When the math was completed and checked, Ms. Eafartaigh returned to the stage for her final announcements. " I am pleased to announce the winners of the Mid-Atlantic Regional Feis. She first mentioned the U-10 winners, but when the first and second place winners were announced in the U-12 group, a cheer went up from the Lincolns. Molly had finished second! And when the final scores were announced for the U-14's, an even larger cheer went up; Maura had finished first in her age group. Both girls would go forward to the North American championship in Canada in late July.

CHAPTER FIVE: CAPE BRETON IN MY DREAMS

The venue emptied quickly, as soon as everyone learned of the potentially massive snowstorm and all of the champions had been announced, After trophies, medals and certificates were awarded to the finalists and the fortunate few posed for photographs. Finally, the dancers retired to the dressing areas and soon were ready to brave the weather outside.

Don Rossi had been monitoring the weather on his cell phone for several hours. "I'm not sure that this storm is going to affect us much at all," he said to Pat. I've been listening to KYW in Philly, and they forecast the storm to slip farther south and slide down into Maryland and the Delmarva Peninsula. If we swing north, there's a strong chance that it won't affect us at all."

"I sure hope you are right. I don't mind snow but its about 33 degrees now, and I hate freezing rain."

The girls, who were ecstatic about their selection to attend the Grand Oireachtas, came bounding down the disused escalator as Pat and Don rushed to the bottom to prevent accidents. "We won, we won!" exclaimed Molly. "I'm so happy! I knew I would have good luck with this dress when I found we had a seven in each of our competitor's numbers. Can I go, daddy, can I go?"

"Hold on, Molly. I have to talk to your mommy and

figure out what we can do. But I wouldn't be surprised if next summer finds you in Nova Scotia!"

"Oh, daddy, you let Maura go to Montreal a few years ago when she won. Please daddy; I want to go to an Oireachtas too!"

At long last, Erin and Annmarie descended the escalator with considerably more care than did the young girls. The fact that both had their arms full of dresses, wigs, dancing shoes and other paraphernalia no doubt played a part. "We're about the last family left up there. One of the security guards had left already, and the other one wanted to get out of here as quickly as she could. I heard her say to one of the mall managers that she lived all the way up above Womelsdorf, and she was afraid of getting stuck on the way home. Little did she know that we had a two-hour ride ahead of us. That's two hours if we're lucky, or heaven knows how long if we're not."

"Well we need to get moving, and get out of here," Pat said. "Although Don has been listening to KYW and they think the storm will head south, let's get out to the car and get rolling. If it doesn't get too bad, we can stop and have a quick dinner somewhere on the Turnpike."

Don was right. The storm did head south, and by the time it was over, it had dumped eight inches of snow on Baltimore. Philadelphia only got a dusting, and north of

Trenton, there was no snow at all. It was a very happy ride home until exhaustion overcame the girls' excitement and they fell asleep and did not awake until they arrived home a few hours later. Everyone was ravishing hungry, but because of the sleeping girls, the adults decided to push on to their destination. After dropping off the Rossi's, the Lincolns arrived home safely, tired but exhilarated from the events of the day.

Life soon returned to normal. Erin pondered whether or not she should order new dancing dresses for both girls. "On the one hand," she thought to herself, "both Maura and Molly love the dresses they have now. On the other hand, the Oireachtas is only six months from now, and heaven knows how much either girl will grow between now and then." In casual conversation with other dance mothers, she asked about sources and current pricing of the top of the line dance costumes. She was not encouraged by what she learned.

Talking to Pat after dinner one evening, she commented "Pat; this whole thing is driving me crazy. I checked, and some of the prices are outrageous! Do you know that there are some studios which charge $2000 or more for a new dress? And even then, very few of them can guarantee delivery in six months or less. There is even one studio in Ireland which does not allow you to choose the design! The designer seems to think he knows better than anyone what would be best for your child! Can you believe that?"

Pat, whose saw his primary role in the world of dance as the chief financial officer of the Lincoln clan, just sighed. "That's a thousand bucks for both dresses?"

"No dear, that's $2000 <u>per dress</u>! And even, then what if we got a dress that Maura or Molly didn't like? I think, given that the girls both love their current dresses, the best thing we can do is to hope they don't grow too much in the next six months. There is still room in the seams for both dresses, and since no one has ever seen them dancing in Nova Scotia, I don't think there will be a problem. What do you think?"

"Well, I'm good with anything you want to do. Realize that we are going to have a fair amount of additional expense just getting to and from Cape Breton. Incidentally, in yesterday's mail, we got a short note from the New England Region saying they were working with the Cape Breton folks to arrange reasonably priced flights and accommodations. I sure hope that works out!"

When Erin discussed dresses with Maura and Molly, they both agreed that they would prefer to dance in their "lucky dresses." After spending Christmas break visiting with their grandparents in Pennsylvania and New York, and having a very peaceful Christmas Day at home, the girls returned to school in January and buckled down for the long semester until summer break.

As happens in many parochial schools, St. Margaret's had an open house/parents night in honor of Catholic School Week in early February. During the open house, Erin spoke to both Maura's and Molly's teachers, and both mentioned that topics for the Diocesan Book Reports had been announced. Molly, in the sixth grade, would be responsible for a book report on world geography; and Maura, being an eighth grader, would be responsible for a paper about Native Americans and other indigenous people. Like many teens and preteens, both had neglected to mention this development to their parents.

After the open house, Erin confronted her daughters. "Hey, you two, what topics are you going to choose for your diocesan book reports this year?" Neither girl had a clue; they, like most kids of their age assumed that something would pop up somewhere.

"OK, then, How about this? Molly, why not write about Cape Breton? There are not a lot of people who know much about it, I bet, in fact, there are probably fairly few people who even know where it's located. Maura, why don't you write about the native peoples who lived there? I don't know much about the place myself, But I bet you can find a good deal of information at the library."

"The library? That's so old school mom; nobody researches at the library anymore. We can find everything we want, I bet, right on the Internet and that way neither you or dad need to drive us across town. Can we try that first, mom?" Erin laughed and conceded.

Shortly after St. Patrick's Day (Always a hectic time for the Irish dancing community!), the Lincolns received another letter from the transportation and housing office, which had arranged discounted charter flights from Boston Logan Airport to Sydney Nova Scotia on Air Canada. For $300 round trip, two chartered Boeing 737 aircraft, each seating 160 passengers, would make three round trips daily starting on Wednesday, July 23, and three trips returning beginning on Thursday, August 1st.Since Pat was out-of-town on a short business trip, Erin researched the flight options to Cape Breton. She first learned that Sydney's Douglas McCurdy Airport (YQY) was quite close to the Oireachtas venue at Cape Breton University. Erin then learned that Air Canada had an excellent safety record and had been flying 737s throughout Canada and the sub-Arctic for the past 25 years. Researching the alternatives, she discovered that the lowest commercial fare (with substantial restrictions) was $366 from Boston and $420 if they chose to leave from LaGuardia. When she spoke to Pat later that evening, she told him what she had learned.

"I think they've come up with a good deal. And the charter flight will take about two hours, nonstop. We hop on at Boston and fly directly to Sydney Nova Scotia with no plane changes. What's not to like?"

"Well, one thing not to like is the drive to Logan Airport. It's about a 3 1/2 hours drive to Boston and then about another hour to get through the "big ditch" and out to Logan. As far as LaGuardia goes, I'd skip that option if we can. Why don't we do this: let's look for the earliest flight into Cape Breton and see if they can get us on that. That will give us a couple of days before the grand opening of the Oireachtas, and we can rent a car and wander around for a while. That will help reduce the nervousness of our girls and give us a chance to see a part of the world that we normally would not see. What do you think, Babe?"

"Well, you know what they say about great minds running in the same circles. That's exactly what I thought too, Pat. I will get a quick email out and reserve the charter flight. The other thing I was thinking about is that Maura and Molly will probably enjoy riding on a plane filled with other dancers from different parts of the USA. I checked different routes such as Chicago – Sydney, and Cincinnati – Sydney and they're all significantly more expensive than this one. There will be dozens of dancers on board, I bet."

"Well you know what we say about sales calls, Erin," Pat said laughing. "When you make the sale, stop talking!" Erin laughed as well. "I get the point, and I'll confirm all this in the morning."

Erin emailed the transportation coordinator and received a speedy reply, confirming the reservation and directing Erin to make payment directly to the organizing committee in Nova Scotia. She also remarked that lodging reservations aboard the small cruise ship, MV TORSHAVN were available at reduced cost, and when Erin contacted the organizing committee directly, she learned that double staterooms were available at C$200 per night. Since there would be four persons in the traveling party, she calculated the total expense as C$400 (~US $295) per night including breakfast and dinner. The Nova Scotia committee also informed her that all ground transportation, including to and from the airport, and transportation to and from the venue would be provided at no cost. Both Erin and Pat were impressed by the organizational competence of the Nova Scotia committee.

There remained only one major obstacle to their participation. Both Erin and Pat laid down the law to Mara and Molly that their school assignments, and particularly their book reports must be completed before they could consider the trip to Nova Scotia a 'done deal.'

And time was getting short. The book reports were due on April 7th, the last day before Easter break. As the frosts of March turned into April showers, Erin returned one afternoon to find stacks of books on the kitchen table. "Where did you get these?" she asked.

"Oh, daddy got them for us from the New York Public Library. We're going to start writing our book reports today!"

"I'll be glad to help," Erin replied, but both girls wanted to do it together. "OK, but you have to let Daddy or me check your work!"

Maura chose "*Rise Again!: the Story of Cape Breton Island*" by Robert J. Morgan, (2008). Molly picked "*Míkmaq: Peoples of the Maritimes*" by Stephen A. Davis, (1998) and just a few days before the papers were due in class, they showed their work to their parents. Both Erin and Pat read the papers eagerly.

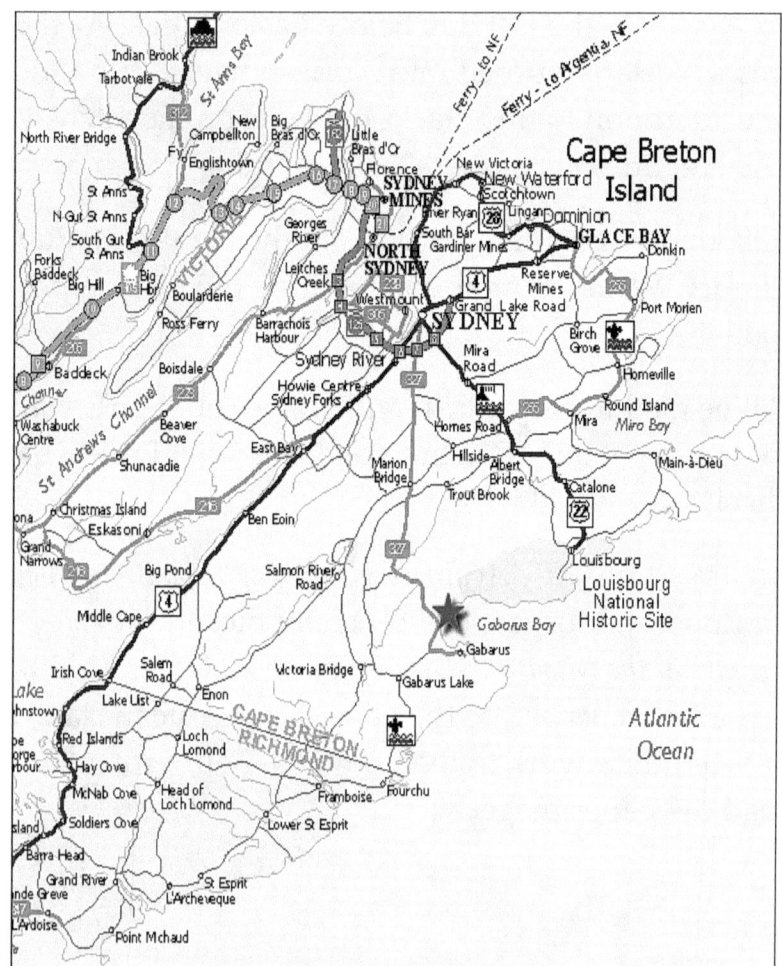

THE ISLAND OF CAPE BRETON, NOVA SCOTIA

CHAPTER SIX: I'M LEAVING ON A JET PLANE

St. Margaret's School

Molly Lincoln

"Rise Again!: the Story of Cape Breton Island"
by Robert J. Morgan

Mr. Morgan says that the 3,981 sq mile island accounts for 18.7% of Nova Scotia's total area. He says the island is east-northeast of the mainland. Its landmass slopes upward from south to north, ending in the highlands of its northern cape. One of the world's larger saltwater lakes, Bras d'Or is in the middle.

There are 132,010 "Cape Bretoners"; about 15% of the provincial population.

John Cabot visited the island in 1497. This discovery is remembered by the Cabot Trail, and by the Cabot's Landing Historic Site & Provincial Park.

In 1521 a lot of people came from Portugal and built a fishing colony on the island. As many as two hundred people lived there and ate fish.

These settlements lasted only one generation. Later, other European settlements were permanently established on the island.

In 1784, Britain split the colony of Nova Scotia into three separate colonies: New Brunswick, Cape Breton Island, and Nova Scotia.

Some people emigrated to the Canadian colonies, like Cape Breton. Shortly after, the mineral rights to the island were given over to the Duke of York instead of New York.

Large-scale shipbuilding began in the 1790s, beginning with schooners for local trade evolving in the 1820s to bigger ships, mostly built for British shipowners.

In 1820, the colony of Cape Breton Island was merged for the second time with Nova Scotia. By the late 19th century, as a result of the faster shipping, expanding fishery and industrialization of the island, exchanges of people between the island of Newfoundland and Cape Breton increased.

During the first half of the 19th century, Cape Breton Island also picked up 50,000 Highland Scots because they had a clearance. Today, the descendants of the Highland Scots dominate Cape Breton Island's culture, particularly in rural communities. They dance jigs, reels, the same dances we do and speak Irish, which they call Garlic. The English don't want them to speak Garlic, though and turned off their televisions. Many of the Scots who immigrated there were either Catholics or Protestants, which can be seen in some island landmarks and place names. They also love to dance and play the fiddle. The world's biggest fiddle is owned by a man named Sydney.

Alexander Graham Bell and Marconi lived in Cape Breton. Alexander Graham Bell lived in Badock because it looked a lot like Scotland. He built a summer cottage where he experimented with deaf people, like Helen Keller—and continued to invent. Bell also built the forerunner to the iron lung and experimented with building sheep.

Marconi's major contributions to Cape Breton included transmitting the first trans-Atlantic radio message from Table Head at Glace Bay to Poldhu England. Marconi's station at the outskirts of Glace Bay became the chief communication center for the Royal Canadian Navy in World War I and the early years of World War II.

Promotions of tourism beginning in the 1950s;

recognizing the importance of the Scottish culture to the province, the provincial government encouraged the use of Garlic some more.

In the 1960s, the Fortress of Louisbourg was partially reconstructed and since 2009, has attracted an average of 90 000 visitors per year. My parents said we could go if we have time.

The Cape Breton Highlands are an extension of the Appalachian mountain. In 1936, the federal government established the Cape Breton Highlands National Park covering366 sq miles across the northern third of the Highlands. The Cabot Trail scenic highway also encircles the plateau's coastal perimeter.

The climate is one of warm summers and cold winters, just like Rockland County. Precipitation can exceed 60 inches on the eastern side facing the Atlantic storms. It snows a lot in the winter, especially in the highlands.

Later migrations of people from Poland, Russia, and Eastern Europeans mostly settled in the island's eastern part around the industrial Cape Breton region. Cape Breton Island's population has been in decline two decades because the old people are dying.

Much of the history of Cape Breton Island involves the coal industry. The island has two major coal deposits:

The Sydney Coal Field in the northeastern part of the island along the Atlantic Ocean drove the Industrial Cape Breton economy, until after World War II.

The Inverness Coal Field in the western part of the island along the Gulf of St. Lawrence is significantly smaller but hosted several mines.

Tourism, in particular, has grown throughout the post-war era and was furthered by the creation of the Cabot Trail scenic drive.

Whale-watching cruises are operated by sailors. The most popular species found in Cape Breton's waters is the Pilot whale. I hope that all my friends can see Cape Breton too some day.

St. Margaret's School

Maura Lincoln

"Mikmaq: Peoples of the Maritimes"

by Stephen A. Davis

The Mi'kmaq are a First Nations people indigenous to Canada's Atlantic Provinces and the northeastern region of Maine. They call their national territory Mi'kma'ki. The nation has a population of about 40,000, of whom nearly 11,000 speak Mi'kmaq, an Eastern Algonquian language. Once written in Mi'kmaq hieroglyphic writing, it is now written using most in Latin.

The Santé Mawiómi, or Grand Council, was the traditional senior level of government for the Mi'kmaq people until Canada passed the Indian Act (1876) to require First Nations to establish representative elected governments. After implementation of the Indian Act, the Grand Council took on a more spiritual function. The Grand Council was made up of chiefs of the seven district councils of Mi'kma'ki.

The Mi'kmaq lived in an annual cycle of seasonal movement between residing in interior winter camps and larger coastal communities during the summer. The spawning runs of March began their movement to converge on smelt spawning streams. They next harvested spawning herring, gathered waterfowl eggs, and hunted geese. By May, the seashore offered abundant cod and shellfish, and coastal breezes brought relief from the biting black flies and mosquitoes of the interior. Autumn frost killed the biting insects during the September harvest of spawning American eels. The most important animal hunted by the Mi'kmaq were moose, of which they used every part: the meat was processed for food, the skin for clothing, tendons, and sinew for cordage, and bones for carving and tools. They also hunted/trapped deer, caribou, bear, rabbit, beaver, porcupine and other small animals.

During this hunt, the men would try to direct the moose in the direction of the camp, so that the women would not have to go as far to drag the moose back. A boy became a man in the eyes of the community after he had killed his first moose. It marked the passage after which he earned the right to marry. They sang a lot and danced in their moccasins.

The Mi'kmaq territory was divided into seven traditional districts. Each district had its independent government and boundaries. The independent governments had a district chief and a council. The council members were band chiefs, elders, and other worthy community leaders.

The Mi'kmaq lived in structures called wigwams. They cut down saplings, which were usually spruce, and curved them over a circle drawn on the ground. These saplings were lashed together at the top and then covered with birch bark. The Mi'kmaq had two different sizes of wigwams. The smaller size could hold 10-15 people and the larger size 15-20 people.

Wigwams could be either conical or domed in shape.

In 1610, people converted to Catholicism and were baptized. They concluded an alliance with the French Jesuits which affirmed the right of Mi'kmaq to choose Catholicism and\or Mi'kmaq traditions.

In 1914, over 150 Mi'kmaq men signed up during World War I. Thirty-four out of sixty-four male Mi'kmaq in the armed forces, distinguished themselves particularly in the Battle of Amiens. In 1939, over 250 Mi'kmaq volunteered in World War II. In 1950, over 60 Mi'kmaq enlisted to serve in the Korean War.

Many Mi'kmaq practice the Catholic faith, some only practice traditional Mi'kmaq religion, while many have adopted both religions. There is one myth explaining that the Mi'kmaq once believed that evil and wickedness among men is what causes them to kill each other. This causes great sorrow to the creator-sun-god, who weeps tears that become rains sufficient to trigger a deluge. The people attempt to survive the flood by traveling in bark canoes, but only a single old man and woman survive to populate the earth. I think they are cool and I hope you do too.

The two girls worked diligently on their book reports over the weekend. After a short disagreement as to who would get to use the printer first, ("I'm the oldest" "But I was ready first!"), Molly brought her book report to her mother for review. Reading slowly through the paper, and trying to maintain a straight face, Erin said, encouragingly "This is excellent work, Molly. But I just wonder, did you run the spell checker on this paper?" Molly nodded affirmatively.

"Well, I think the spell checker may have misunderstood what you're trying to say," Erin said as gently as she could."You have the people of Cape Breton speaking Garlic; I think what you really mean is that they speak Gaelic. You'll have to change that before you turn this into Mrs. Nelson. But all in all is an excellent book report, Molly!"

While she read Molly's paper, Pat read Maura's just as carefully. "You certainly had some difficult words and terms here, Maura. Did you copy them directly from the book?" Maura also nodded affirmatively. "Well on an a book report in grade school that's okay, I guess, but you really ought to try to paraphrase a bit more. Just take the words that the author wrote and change them into your own words while trying to keep the same message. You'll have to paraphrase when you get to high school and college, Maura! But this is a good paper, and you can turn it in tomorrow to Ms. Hanlon, and I think she will like it a lot. You took some difficult material and made it quite understandable."

Both girls received excellent grades and encouraging comments on the book reports from their teachers. "Wow," said Maura to Molly during recess, "that's one big obstacle out of the way, and we should be good to go for the Grand Oireachtas." I know this is your first and you're really going to enjoy it, let me tell you!"

As the departure day approached in mid-July, Erin received some troubling news from the other dance-mothers in the Tri-State Academy. She learned that Sinaed DiPero was forced to withdraw from the Grand Oireachtas, due to her mother's grave illness. "I think it must be cancer," Erin told Pat that evening. "I can't think of anything else that would cause poor little Sinaed DiPero to have to withdraw. She finished a solid second after Maura. She must be devastated. I understand that the third-place finisher will take her place."

Maura was distraught when she learned that Annie Riley of York's Trinity Gaelic Dance School would take her place.

"Oh, mom, not Annie. She is a really really nasty girl. She lords it over everyone because she is a star at her dancing school and always compares her dress, which her mother bought for her in Ireland, with everyone's. She really bullies everyone that dances with her. I wish that Sinaed DiPero was able to go, she's really nice kid. This is really a bummer, you know?" Erin comforted her eldest daughter. "Some things just can't be helped, Maura."

But at last, departure day arrived and very early that Wednesday morning, they packed the car and began the tedious drive to Boston Logan Airport. Once on Interstate 84 however, things went smoothly, and they arrived well ahead of their 2 PM scheduled charter flight. There were dozens of dancers, parents, and other relatives milling around Logan's Terminal B for their trip, but volunteers from the Old Colony Dance Academy had things well in hand, and they boarded the 737 a few minutes before 2PM. It was open seating, and most of the dancers sat together, while the grownups made do with what was left. The flight went smoothly and arrived shortly after 5 PM.

CHAPTER SEVEN: SHE'S CALLED NOVA SCOTIA

After a very happy (some might say raucous) trip, the 737 landed on time at Sydney airport. "Fifty young kids, sitting together can make a lot of noise on an airplane," Erin said to Pat. "Who knew that teenage step dancers knew so many songs and could sing so well?" Pat, a bit stiff from fitting his 6'4 frame into a seat in the economy section, just laughed. "We do a lot for our kids, Erin, but I take can't too much more of this. I'm glad we've landed!"

There was another pleasant surprise in store. When they reached the baggage claim area, they found a portable stage installed just a few yards from the luggage conveyors. There, young dancers from the Glace Bay Dance Academy performed jigs, reels and Highland step dancing to the delight of the arriving passengers. "They certainly have this well-organized," Erin said. "This looks like it is going to be an excellent experience not only for our kids but for us." Pat, who had worked out the kinks in his legs on the walk from the arrival gate to the baggage claim area smiled. "I'm sure it will," said he.

After they had gathered their bags, they encountered a young woman holding a sign: 'Grand Oireachtas Participants.' She guided them to a large anteroom, where tea, coffee, and fruit juices, as well as healthy snacks, were waiting. "Please see Angus in the back of the room, and he'll place tags with your stateroom number on every bag. Because we'll be riding regular school buses down to the cruise pavilion, we'll transfer the bags in a separate truck. And have no fear, we're all dance-parents too; the dresses and other valuables will be safe with us. Now, if we're all here, please follow me to the buses." There, waiting with engines idling were five school buses, and two large trucks ready to take the passenger and their luggage to their accommodations on the MV TORSHAVN.

The dancers and their parents boarded the buses in an orderly fashion, and as each bus was loaded, it departed for the short trip to the Sydney waterfront. The buses pulled up on Esplanade Street just a few yards from the gangway of the large and modern ocean-going ship. Pat whistled under his breath. "I was expecting something between a garbage's scow and a tugboat," he said to Erin. "But this is a very nice ship!" The girls, having their first look at an ocean-going vessel were also suitably impressed.

Check-in procedures were a breeze; they just showed the smiling Icelandic purser their airline tickets for the charter flight, and within a few minutes a steward had them safely in their stateroom. And, from the perspective of the girls, the best treat was still in store; he then took of them next door and showed them their full-sized connecting stateroom. "All you have to do, young ladies, is to open this side door, which will connect you directly to your parent's room. There is no need for you to go out in the corridor to get there!" After refreshing themselves for a moment or two, the Lincoln family gathered in their parent's stateroom. "Wow mom, we even have our own private telephone number. We can exchange phone numbers with some of the other girls we met on the flight, and we can talk among ourselves. Let's explore the ship!," said Molly.

"Now, just slow down for a minute. It's nearly 6:30, and I for one am getting hungry," said Pat. "Let's explore together and see if we can find something to eat. They left the stateroom and asked a passing steward where dinner was being served. He directed them to the main restaurant on the seventh deck and showed them to the elevator. When they arrived at the dining room, there was a short line of other parents and dancers, many of whom they recognized from their flight. They were seated at a table for twelve with two other families, one from Maine and the other from Rhode Island, and enjoyed an excellent choice of entrees, skillfully prepared in the ship's galley. "This has to be the best Oireachtas I've ever seen," exclaimed Maura, chatting with her newest dancing friends. This is so cool!"

After dinner and a stroll around the surprisingly spacious vessel, the girls exchanged telephone numbers with their new friends. "We're going to have to set some ground rules here, Pat," Erin said. "Otherwise we'll be hearing the phone ringing from the other stateroom all night, and none of us will get any sleep."

"Well, I've got one or two things I need to do before I turned in," Pat said. I've set up reservations for a car for tomorrow morning through the Tilden Car Agency here in Sydney. They are the Canadian branch of National Car Rentals, and I need to find their offices and then bring the car back to somewhere where I can park it. I did notice that there are some parking lots not far from here, and I think there is an underground parking garage right near the pavilion. Have you given any thought as to where you would like to go tomorrow, Erin?"

"Well, if it were up to me I'd like to see the Cabot Trail around the northwest corner of the island. But I'm afraid that would be boring for Maura and Molly. It just would be three or four hours in the car looking at mountains, valleys, and the ocean. I don't think there is an amusement park or water park or anything like that close by, but I read that Fortress Louisbourg is a great destination for young kids. Why don't you find out how far it is and how long it might take to get there and back, Pat."

After an excellent breakfast on the Odin deck (the open air dining area at the ship's stern), Pat left Erin and the kids to explore the ship at greater length while he went to the Tilden Agency to retrieve his rental car. He was surprised when they offered him a very low mileage Hyundai Santa Fe. He signed the contract and drove the short distance down Esplanade Street and found the underground parking area as expected. He re-boarded the ship, and found Erin and the girls in their suite, unpacking their dancing costumes. "Well," Pat said, "I have the car, and I'm ready to go. The question is, to where?"

Erin responded. "While we were wandering around, I picked up some brochures, and I think that we would enjoy the living history museum at Fortress Louisbourg. I know I would, and It looks like it's a short drive from here. I think we would all learn something about Cape Breton. Here, Pat take a look at the little map on the last page of the brochure. It looks like it's just down N.S. 22 from here and it shouldn't take us more than an hour to get there."

The girls returned to their stateroom and changed into their casual clothes. Erin and Pat got ready, and by 10 AM they were all in the car en route to Louisbourg. Erin read from the brochure to her now captive audience:

"The Fortress of Louisbourg has been the most significant reconstruction project in North America. The settlement was founded in 1713 by the French and developed over several

decades into a thriving center for fishing and trade. Louisbourg was besieged twice before finally being destroyed in the 1760s. The site lay untouched until well into modern times when archaeologists began to reconstruct the fortress as it was in the 18th century.

Thanks to Parks Canada, you can now experience life in Louisbourg during its heyday. There are more than a dozen buildings open to the public, including three authentic working 18th-century restaurants while hundreds of re-enactors or "animators" of all age populate the streets of the restored fortress; working, playing, and living life as they would have in 1744."

A half hour later, they were inside the vast fortress and ready to experience eighteenth century Cape Breton. There were certainly lots of things to do and see. There were soldiers and civilians, men, women, and children all reenacting what their daily lives must have been like nearly three hundred years before. There were a dozen or more buildings to explore too; a working forge and blacksmith shop, restaurants, stables, and farmhouses, as well as the homes of the gentry. Soldiers paraded and fired muskets and cannons, and both girls, as well as their parents, found it immensely entertaining. There were even animals, and Molly took the opportunity to pet a small piglet in the stable areas. And there was a gift shop: (There is always a gift shop!), and Maura and Molly stocked up on trinkets to share with their friends when school resumed in the fall.

It was late in the day when they finally returned to Sydney. The first thing they noticed when they arrived aboard the ship was that several additional planeloads of dancers and their families had arrived. At dinner that evening they sat with three new families, who had just arrived from Chicago, Denver, and Nashville. "Boy this Grand Oireachtas is really something," Molly remarked. "You haven't seen anything yet," replied Maura. "Wait until tomorrow when it actually begins. You'll see Irish dancers from all over the world!." While they were enjoying dinner that evening, ship's stewards slid two-page information packets under each stateroom door. When they returned, Erin retrieved their copy, scanned it and passed it to Pat.

Pat reviewed the information too and announced, "OK, listen up kids, this is important. Breakfast tomorrow will be served from 6:30 AM to 9 AM only, and we have to be ready to board buses for Cape Breton University no later than 10:30 AM. It says here that all dancers should be wearing the dress they intend to wear to compete, and that all dancers will gather by age groups at the seats on the main floor of the Parker MacDonald Auditorium where the opening ceremony will take place. Mom and I will sit with parents and friends in the stands." (The newly refurbished Parker MacDonald Multi-Purpose Assembly Hall at CBU's Canada Games Complex honored Parker MacDonald, the first and most famous son of Cape Breton to play in the National Hockey League.)

He continued reading. " The opening ceremony will begin precisely at noon and will take about sixty minutes to complete. The only dancing tomorrow afternoon will be noncompetitive for the very youngest dancers, all of whom represent local dance academies, These U-6, U-8 and U-10 will 'fun-dance' in appreciation of their hard work, just to give them a taste of the competitive environment. The official Oireachtas will begin at 10 AM Sunday, with the final Parade of Champions on Wednesday afternoon. So everyone, let's get a good night's sleep because tomorrow is going to be a hectic day."

The girls woke even before their alarms sounded. Erin could sense the excitement that Maura and Molly were feeling already. They washed and dressed, and still in their casual clothing went down to the Odin deck for breakfast. It was clear that they were not the only excited dancers aboard the ship. Maura and Molly found two of their new friends and sat with them while Pat and Erin relaxed with a friendly young couple from Ft. McMurray AB. They chatted and lingered for a moment or two over coffee, while the Albertans shared their experiences of the day before.

"We had always wanted to see the Miner's Museum here in Glace Bay, but when we got there, we found that it was undergoing renovations and would not be open again until August 15. We were disappointed because both of our parents are from the Maritimes, but we went to Plan B and took our Caitlin to Fortress Louisbourg. That was fun, but it would've been more fun, I suppose, had we been able to get into the Miner's Museum." Both couples shared their impressions of the fortress and then gathered their dancers and returned to the staterooms to dress.

Well before the scheduled departures, everyone gathered at the 'quarterdeck' adjacent to the gangway. At about 9:45, one of the volunteers announced that the buses were staged just north of the pier, and the buses would load in front of the pavilion. She also announced that they would dispatch 120 passengers at a time for boarding, which was the capacity of three school buses.

Boarding began promptly at 10 AM. Police officers were on hand to hold traffic as groups of participants crossed Esplanade Street to the pavilion and boarded for the short trip to the University. All in all, it was an incredibly efficient transportation service, thanks in part to the preplanning of Constabulary Staff Sgt. Morrison and Mr. Breslin of the school board. By 11:30 AM, all of the dancers were seated on the main floor of the MacDonald arena, while their family and friends were sitting in the surrounding grandstands.

Promptly at noon, the Honourable Sandra Miller, the planning chairperson, called everyone to attention. After a brief welcoming speech, she invited Bishop Patrick Manning of the Roman Catholic Diocese of Antigonish to deliver the invocation. The bishop was mercifully brief, and then the chairperson introduced The Premier Of Nova Scotia, Alex Henderson, who again welcomed everyone to the province. The last official to speak was George Hamlin, Mayor Of The Cape Breton Municipal Authority who added his greetings, and at long last Algernon Worthington-Smythe DD, the Anglican Archbishop of Nova Scotia offered a prayer for the safety of all participants.

At that point, with a reminder to all participants to check their schedules carefully for times and stage locations around the sprawling campus, the meeting adjourned until 1:30 PM at which time the kiddie dancers would perform for their parents and friends. The Lincoln family rejoined the very orderly departure to the school buses and returned to the ship to prepare for their big day tomorrow.

THE JOAN HARRISS WELCOME CENTER,SYDNEY NS

M.V.TORSHAVEN ENTERING SYDNEY HARBOUR

CHAPTER EIGHT: GIRLS JUST WANNA HAVE FUN

After they had returned to the ship and changed into more comfortable clothes, Maura and Molly approached their parents with a proposal. "Say, Dad, a lot of our friends are going to go exploring the ship again. Can Molly and I go too?"

"Aw, Maura, your mom and I are both exhausted. Riding with your knees tucked up against your chin on a packed school bus is something we haven't done in years, and to be honest with you, it's not something I look forward to. Can't you guys just take a rest and see what's on the TV in your room?"

"Dad, we've seen everything there is to be seen on this Canadian television network. It looks like they've only got three stations! And my cell phone doesn't work here anymore, so I can't play any games online. Please, daddy, let us go with our friends!"

"Maybe later, Maura. I'm going to lie down for a quick nap," Erin interjected.

"Well, mom we didn't expect you to come along with us. It's just a couple of girls that we've met since we got here and we promise, mom, we really, really promise we won't go off the ship. Please, mom!"

Erin frowned and looked at Pat who also frowned. "I'm

not sure this is a good idea at all, Maura. But if you promise not to leave the ship and stay out of any place you are not supposed to go and you stay with your friends, I suppose you can go for a little while. But listen to me, Maura, you have to keep Molly with you at all times. Is that clear?" Both girls nodded affirmatively.

"And you know what that means it don't you, Maura? If Molly wants to hang around with her friends who are under twelve, and you want to go hang around with your older friends, you're going to have to hang around with the younger girls, is that clear?"

Both girls nodded affirmatively but with somewhat less enthusiasm. "It's now about 3 PM. I want you back here ready to go to dinner at 5 PM, is that perfectly clear? And if your dad and I decide to take a walk around the promenade deck, and we see you guys in any place you shouldn't be, the next time you get to play around with a boat will be in the bathtub. Now go and have some fun!"

Both girls realized that they had won the battle, if not necessarily the war. Both scurried back to their stateroom, and after a short squabble as to who would make the first phone calls, Molly called several of her friends and agreed to meet on the quarterdeck adjacent to the gangway. Maura did the same, and soon after, the two adventuresses were wandering around with a group of dancers of all ages.

They were not, by far, the only group of girls exploring the ship on their own, They began to take on the characteristics of a 'flash mob'; the group would expand or collapse as new kids joined and then broke off. The ship's stewards, realizing that exerting any form of control would probably cause a mutiny, retreated to a service alley and watched a soccer match on CBC television.

The girls, not recognizing that they were, in effect, in charge of an oceangoing liner, explored from stem to stern, from bilge to smokestack and everywhere they could go without being stopped by a chain bearing a 'DO NOT ENTER' sign. They crossed the quarterdeck several times, and once when Maura and Molly were in between 'flash mobs' overheard a distressing conversation between a mother and one of the volunteers who was coordinating activities on the ship.

"What the hell do you mean that we're going to ride back and forth on school buses? I just spent two days driving up here from Pennsylvania! We spent last night in a crummy motel in some place called Moncton, and now we're on this fleabag boat, and we're going to be riding school buses all over this place. When I get home to America, you can be sure that I'm going to complain to everybody about the way you Canucks are treating us!"

Her daughter, holding what was apparently her dance

costume in a tattered garment bag, interjected. "Come on mom, let's go to our room and sit down and rest for a while." The woman turned and scowled at her daughter. "You keep out of this Annie if you know what's good for you. You just let me talk to this lady here about the way we're being treated." Annie, the daughter, just sighed quietly.

Maura and Molly continued their explorations until a quick glance at a clock indicated the time was 4:30 PM. "Whoops," Molly said, "time for us to get back to the room. But it sure is fun to explore a ship like this without mom and dad looking over our shoulders! I may even join the Navy, just like Uncle John someday," Maura looked at her sister as if she were slightly crazy, but both began to make their way back to their stateroom.

As they entered the passageway leading to their room, they could hear a disturbance in one of the staterooms further down the corridor. They stopped and listened for a moment and then hurried back to their room. Erin and Pat were waiting for them.

"Well, you were very trustworthy! Your dad and I did go for a long walk around the promenade deck, and while we saw lots of girls running and being a nuisance, we didn't see you or your friends. Did you have fun?"

"Yes we did," Maura replied. "But you know what, there

was some lady really yelling at the volunteer coordinator down by the place where we get aboard the ship. She really was mean, and when we were coming back and turned the corner from the elevator, we could hear her yelling at her daughter in their room. It was so loud that even with the door closed we could hear her shouting and her daughter crying and honest to God mom, it sounded like she gave her a very hard smack. The girl started crying louder, but Molly and I didn't want to be a caught listening, and so we just came back here."

Erin looked on with concern. "Do you have any idea who it was, Maura?" Molly replied instead. "I heard her say she drove up from Pennsylvania and that they stayed in a motel last night. But I didn't recognize her, or her daughter except her daughter looks like she may have been about Maura's age." Pat and Erin looked at each other with concern but said nothing. "Well you girls stay away from them, whoever they might be," Pat said. "And if anyone says mean things to you, you come and tell me immediately okay? Now I for one am starving so let's go and change again and head up to the restaurant, shall we?"

They arrived at dinner, and since everyone was now aboard, the lines to the restaurant were longer than ever. While in the queue Molly and Maura spotted a few of their adventurous friends, and ask if they could sit together at a separate table. When Pat and Erin finally made it to the front of the line, they found themselves in a group with five other couples sitting quite close to the galley door. Their new friends from Alberta were there, but everyone else had just arrived, and after a round of introductions they settled down to their hors-d'oeuvres and pre-dinner drinks.

One couple, the Kennedys from Harrisburg, had also participated in the King Of Prussia Feis. As it turned out, they were the parents of the one dancer who had outscored Molly in the U-12 age group. They exchanged pleasantries, and Erin asked Mary Kennedy if she knew the Riley's of York, just a few miles away from Harrisburg.

"Oh, you must mean Tonya Riley. She's a single parent, and I think she has a 13-year-old. I think she said that she was going to drive up here. Personally, the thought of a drive for two whole days just to get here when you could fly seems sort of loony to me, but I understand from other mothers who know her that they're pretty well strapped for cash. I've actually never met her, but the people with whom her daughter Annie dances say that she is fanatical about Annie doing well in competitions. I don't know why that would be; Gawd knows there is no money in this, but maybe she thinks that someday Annie will be able to perform in Riverdance or some other

Broadway production. She probably would have a better chance of hitting the lottery, though." Erin nodded but kept her revelations to herself.

Once again, the dinner was excellent, and when the parents had finished, they went to collect their girls from the two tables where the 'Torshavn Terrors' had collected. Once back in their stateroom, they found a large packet of information that had been delivered by their steward. While Pat stood on the state-room balcony, watching the sunset over Cape Breton, Erin perused and jotted notes on the side of the dance schedule. She called Maura and Molly back into the family stateroom. Pat came in from the balcony to listen.

"Okay gang, listen up because this is important. Not only do I have the stage schedule but I have a listing of which tunes will accompany you.

First up, they've arranged religious services for tomorrow. Tomorrow is Sunday, remember? It says here that Mass will be celebrated at 9:30 AM in the Broadmore Playhouse. A non-denominational Protestant service will also be celebrated at the same time at the RBC Centre. I wonder what RBC means?" she said to Pat. "Royal Bank Of Canada, Erin" Pat replied. She just shrugged. "Now here's the critical part. Molly listened closely.

Under 12 Schedule:

Venue: Climate Controlled Soccer Dome

Round 1: All Inclusive 30 DANCERS (Group C)

Sunday Stage J 11:20 AM: *Blue Eyed Rascal: Kilkenny Races:* [Top 25 Dancers Advance]

Round 2 Stage I 1:45 PM *Jig: Storyteller: St. Patrick's Day:*

[Top 20 Dancers Advance]

Round 3 Stage L 3:45 PM *Garden Of Daisies; Sprig Of Shillelagh:* 6-10 [Top 15 Dancers Advance]

Round 4 Stage K 5:15 PM *Modern Jig Set* [Top 10 Dancers Advance]

Note: =5= Dancers Will Drop After Each Of Four Rounds and

Top 5 Dancers Advance To U-14 Semi-Finals on Stage B Monday at 10:30 AM

Maura, here's your schedule: You are dancing at the MacDonald Arena where we were today.

Under 14 Schedule:

Round 1: All Inclusive 30 DANCERS

Group B:

Sunday Stage D 11:10AM *Battle of Arklow*: Lodge *Road:* [Top 25 Dancers Advance]

Round 2 Stage G 1:15 PM *Deep Green Pool: Hurry the Jug:* [Top 20 Dancers Advance]

Round 3 Stage F 3:30 PM *King of the Fairies: Miss Brown's Fancy:* [Top 15 Dancers Advance]

Round 4 Stage E 5:00 PM *Modern Jig Set* [Top 10 Dancers Advance]

Note: 5 Dancers Will Drop After Each Of Four Rounds

Top 10 To Semi-Finals – All Groups Stage B Monday 1:00 Pm

" It looks like we're going to have to split up again, at least for tomorrow,Pat. The good news is that there's plenty of time after Mass to get to the dancing venues. "But once we get going, it looks like the interval between sessions is fairly short, and we will be through the qualifying stages by the time we come back tomorrow afternoon. The real work starts on Monday if we make it to the semifinals. They are not announcing the musical selections for the semifinals in advance."

"Okay, you guys got that? We're going to have to be up super early tomorrow, to get breakfast on the Odin deck, mainly because 1200 other people or more will be trying to do it at the same time. Then we'll head out to Mass, and tomorrow is really the big day! Okay, you two get over to your room and get cleaned up; you both smell like diesel oil from your adventures and get a good nights sleep. And do not -- repeat do not --make any telephone calls to the other girls, and if you get any calls just ignore them. Wake up time tomorrow is going to be about 6 AM!

CHAPTER NINE: SHE WELCOMES THE STRANGERS

Autumn comes early to Cape Breton, and when they awoke shortly after 6 AM the outside temperature was a crisp 53°F. By 7:00 they were ready to go to the Odin deck for breakfast, and Erin insisted that they all wear sweaters to ward off the chill. After a quick breakfast, they returned to the staterooms and prepared for the first dancing day of the Grand Oireachtas.

They boarded a small 24 passenger bus shortly before 8:30 AM, and after a very quick trip, made even more pleasant by the entertaining and informative patter of Rudy, their driver, and with little traffic on the roads at that hour arrived at the Boardmore Playhouse shortly before Mass was scheduled to begin. Msgr. John J. McKenna, assisted by Deacon Bob Monahan clebrated. After a short homily, and special prayers for Dominic Francis Rotella, a parishioner who had died from a long lingering illness, at the conclusion of Mass Deacon Bob wished all of the dancers the best of luck and processed back to the sacristy. When they had left the Broadmore Playhouse, Pat and Erin debated 'who would go where.' "If it's okay with you, Pat, I'll accompany Maura to her first two sessions," she said, hoping that there would indeed be two or more sessions today for her oldest daughter. "Why don't you go with Molly, and we can swap out again at "halftime". Pat, agreed, and he and Molly began the short walk across campus to the large enclosed Soccer Dome. They were surprised at how large it was; there were two championship-sized playing fields back-to-back, and four large stages, one in each corner of the playing area. Every stage was surrounded by a semicircle of about 150 padded folding chairs. Each stage was about 6 feet high,and each had a different ten-foot high backdrop designed and painted by art students from the University.

Stage J, where Molly would begin the preliminary trials sported a giant montage of coal miners from 18th to 21st century Cape Breton. While Pat waited for the dancing to start, he wandered around and looked at the other backdrops. Stage I featured fisherman and lobstermen working in the offshore waters of the island, while Stage K featured several scenes from the lives of the Mi'kmaq nation, the original inhabitants of Cape Breton. The last stage was an abstract painting and Pat had to study it for several seconds to realize it was a representation of the student-artists' views of the future of Cape Breton Island. Supersonic aircraft, wireless towers, and even what appeared to be a high-speed railway were featured in the painting. All in all, these backdrops provided a festive atmosphere for the dancers and their guests, and Pat was suitably impressed.

When the 30 participants in group C, just one of eight groups of dancers in the U-12 category were all assembled, an Oireachtas volunteer announced the pairings for the first round, selected randomly by computer. Molly was paired with young Chloe Maguire of Dallas, Texas. They would dance fifth in the rotation of 15 pairs. Pat returned to their stage and took a seat at the end of the third row. The first four pairs danced, (and very well thought Pat, who admittedly knew very little about competitive dancing.) He then became extremely attentive when Molly and Chloe entered the stage.

Their first tune 'Blue Eyed Rascal' was very energetic, and Pat was impressed by both dancers, although he thought that Chloe perhaps had the advantage, since she was both taller and somewhat older than Molly. In the second dance, the 'Kilkenny Races,' a tune to which Molly had danced several times before in local competitions, Pat thought that she had the advantage. But as they bowed and left the stage, Pat had no idea how the adjudicators had judged the performance.

When all 15 pairs of dancers had performed the first round, there was a short intermission followed by an announcement of the 25 dancers who would compete in the second round. (Out of courtesy to all of the dancers, no one announced who had been "dropped," they merely announced those who would proceed to the next round.)

Pat had a chance to chat with Molly in the staging area and congratulated her on her excellent performance.

The volunteer announced that the second round would commence shortly and that Molly and Ellie Nolan of Denver would dance in the third position. Once again Pat, who was rapidly learning what good Irish dancing should look like, watched the first two rounds carefully, and then sat attentively as Molly and Ellie entered the stage. This time it was clear, at least to Pat, that Molly had the advantage over Ellie who appeared to be quite young and was tentative in her steps as they performed two very energetic slip jigs: the *'Storyteller,'* and *'St. Patrick's Day'*, both of which were trendy and familiar to Molly, who had danced them since she had begun at the Tri-State Academy several years previously. When all pairs had completed, Pat waited anxiously for the announcement of those who would go forward. Both he and Molly were delighted to learn that she had made the second cut as well.

During the long dinner break, Pat approached Molly, hugged her tightly and said. "It's time for me to swap out with your mom. She'll be over here before you start the third round. Good luck Molly!"

Pat caught sight of Erin on the pathway between the two venues. As he approached her, he saw that she was visibly shaken. "What happened, Erin? Did Maura have a problem?"

"No, Maura is fine. But there was a real problem during the last dance. That Reilly girl was dancing alongside a girl from British Colombia. And on the second dance, she actually got very, very close to the Canadian dancer. In fact, I'm certain she actually barged into her as they crossed the stage. When the number concluded, the adjudicators ruled it an intentional 'barge,' and all hell broke loose. Her mother, who had been sitting a few rows behind me came charging up to the stage like a cow on steroids. She berated both of the adjudicators, one of whom had nothing at all to do with the decision, and I thought they were going to have to call the police. She was obscene, irate and totally out of control. In all my years of dancing and all the years that our kids have been involved, I never saw anything like it. If there is one unbreakable rule, it's that you never, ever talk to the adjudicators. Luckily, staffers were taping the entire preliminary group activities, and they have an official tape of what occurred. But right now she's out. And if I see the Riley mother anywhere, keep me away from her."

"Oh, and by the way, Maura aced her first two sessions, the first with a girl from Atlanta, I believe, and the second one with a girl from Buffalo. But talk about throwing a wet blanket atop a fun event!"

"Well, Erin, that sort of ties in with what we heard from

our kids last night. Apparently, this Riley woman, whoever she may be, is very tightly wound. I'd be concerned for the daughter, truth to tell."

"Me too. But it was right there in front of at least 100 people, many of whom I believe were from the local dancing academies, so if someone has to make a report, I believe it probably has been made already. But I don't want to go to the dining hall for lunch, in case I run across her there."

"Well, on the side of the Soccer Dome, I saw a paved area, and I believe there are several food trucks there. It's probably set up for the University employees, or maybe even the volunteers, but if we stand in line and pay with Canadian loonies or toonies, no one should be the wiser. We'll keep our kids out of sight until we get the food, and there are a grove of trees with picnic tables behind the arena itself where we can eat in peace."

"Sounds like a plan, Patrick. You're always good at finding ways to solve problems. I bet you didn't think we'd have this particular problem when we came up here. I'll go back and fetch Maura before she heads to the dining hall; you get Molly, and head to the grove of trees behind the venue. We can look at the food trucks then and decide what we want for lunch."

Both parents retrieved their 'assigned' child and a few

minutes later met behind the Soccer Dome. Pat counted six different food trucks offering a wide range of meals. As Erin and the girls remained at the picnic table, Pat went up and encountered a middle-aged fellow, with gray hair in a ponytail, and said to himself "if he's not a university professor I don't know who is." He hailed the professor and said, " Hello, we're new here! What's good?" The professor immediately identified Pat as being attached to the Oireachtas and laughed. "Well if you're not from around here, I would suggest the lobster salad. And if you are from around here, well, you probably wouldn't be asking, but then again you wouldn't want to eat more lobster at lunchtime! For us Nova Scotians lobster it's incredibly cheap, and usually fresh caught and tastes wonderful. Most folks in CB would have it for three meals a day if they had a chance!"

Erin and the girls were delighted when Pat returned with four orders of lobster salad. While there were some places in Cape Breton where lobster salad was a lot more 'salad' than 'lobster,' this particular food truck wasn't one of them. The paper containers were full of lobster pieces, surrounded by just a few vegetables to complete the salad. Erin spoke up. "What would you guys like to drink? I'll go over, and I can get drinks from any of the food trucks here. The one on the far end seems to have the shortest line. Coffee, tea, soft drinks, you guys decide."

After a little prompting from their mother, and a reminder that carbonated drinks might tend to reappear when dancing vigorously, both girls opted for lemonade, and Pat and Erin, getting into the true spirit of Cape Breton opted for Red Rose tea. The weather had warmed a bit, and they spent a pleasant half hour consuming the excellent lobster salad with their drinks. "If this is what Cape Breton food is like," said Maura. "I'm going to move here when I graduate from high school and see if I can attend Cape Breton University!" As they rose to clear the tables, Erin said "Time for us to swap, Pat. If I see that woman again, I'm liable to slug her." Pat agreed and accompanied Maura back to the MacDonald Arena.

They arrived there with plenty of time to spare. Pat sat with Maura on the folding chairs, and it was clear that the events of the morning had disturbed Maura as well. "Look, kiddo, you had nothing to do with that. In fact, you were not even on the stage at the time. I know you're upset, but you've come a long way to make it this far; try to put it behind you. Your mom said you did very well in the first two sessions, now try to stay focused if you can for the remaining two. Know that I will be here with you and cheer you on, and I promise I won't try to beat up on any of the judges!"

Maura just laughed, kissed her Dad, and it was clear that she was getting back into the swing of things.

When the volunteer called the audience to order, she announced that after a review of the videotape, while clearly showed the 'barging' it did not prove whether or not it was intentional, and so the adjudicators had penalized the dancer by 15 points but allowed her to continue. A gasp went up from everyone who had seen the previous event. The volunteer went on to list the dance order for the third session; Maura was paired with Cara Byrne of Calgary Alberta. They would dance in the sixth set of the remaining group of U-14 dancers. Pat took a seat in the last row of the audience, partially to get a better view at the elevated stage, but also to have a view of everyone in front of him.

When Maura and her partner were called the musicians began playing 'King of the Fairies' followed by 'Miss Brown's Fancy,' and when the points were calculated at the completion of the third round, once again Maura had gone through to the fourth and final round of the day. "I wish my cell phone worked here in Canada," Pat said to Maura during the intermission. "I'd like to share the good news with your mom." "Let's keep her in suspense a while longer dad," said Maura jokingly. "Now if I make it through the final round here today, then we can tell her."

And make it through she certainly did! The fourth and final round saw Maura paired with Mia Flynn of Cincinnati. Both young women danced their hearts out, and when the section was completed, it took the adjudicators several additional minutes of consultation to determine who would go forward. But when the announcement was made, there was a gasp from the audience. Maura, of course, went forward but so did Annie Riley. Clearly, the audience was not impressed that the Riley girl had earned enough points after the incident to make it through to the semifinals.

They all met up as previously agreed at the bus stop outside the Soccer Dome. They could tell by Molly running to greet and hug them that she too had qualified to go to the semifinal round the next morning. And it was a very joyful family indeed who return on the school bus to a very happy evening aboard the MV TORSHAVN.

CHAPTER TEN: DARK AS A DUNGON

In the Canadian Maritimes, if you don't like the weather wait a few minutes and it's sure to change. And change it did! While the weather had been pleasant during the first days of the Grand Oireachtas, things changed late Sunday night and Monday morning. The remnants of Hurricane Becky arrived off the coast of Nova Scotia and Cape Breton in the late evening. Although significantly weakened by the colder waters of the Labrador Current, nevertheless it brought winds of forty-five miles per hour or more, and intermittent heavy rains.

Both Erin and Pat were awakened by the storm during the night. Erin commented to Pat, "it's really beginning to blow out there. I hope it doesn't cause any problems getting the girls to the semifinals." Pat groggily replied, "The volunteers been so helpful about everything else, I suppose that they'll have things well under control." And with that, he rolled over and went back to sleep.

Meanwhile, MV Torshavn's First Officer Steni Gunthersssdottir, and Captain Orsteinn Magnusson, both Icelanders with vast experience in northern waters, had directed their crew to add additional mooring lines at the bow and the stern of the vessel. They also deployed small kedge anchors on the starboard side of the ship to increase its holding power in the relatively deep channel. While it may come as a surprise to most 'landlubbers', experienced seamen would much prefer to ride out the heavy weather at sea, rather than at the dock. The captain and his first officer were no exception.

Erin's alarm rang at 6 AM. She glanced out the stateroom window to the balcony and saw that the heavy rain had diminished slightly. Wakening Pat and the girls, they dressed again in casual clothes and went off in search of breakfast. As they expected, there was a small sign at the side of the elevator stating that the Odin deck was closed and that breakfast was available in the main dining room. When they arrived there, they were among the first arrivals and had a table to themselves.

After a hearty breakfast, and returning for a quick steam pressing of the girl's dresses, they departed for the gangway.

They were stopped on the quarterdeck by a rather drenched volunteer, who informed them of a change in plans, and that everyone would remain in the Pavilion until the rains slowed. Other volunteers, wearing neon safety vests over plastic ponchos, and carrying large golf umbrellas, met them at the foot of the gangway and escorted them across to the Pavilion. The assembly areas were crowded with families awaiting transportation to the venue, and in the distance Erin could clearly hear a woman, no doubt the now infamous Tonya Riley, berating all and sundry as if they had some control over the weather.

A few minutes later, a volunteer stood behind the podium and announced. "We're sorry about the weather; this had not been forecasted, but here it is. Also, we've just learned of a minor traffic accident which is blocking Grand Lake Rd. It has been suggested to us that we give the young ladies who are performing in the semifinals precedence in boarding the buses, and that family members can follow along a few minutes later. This change should help the organizers of the event keep as close to schedule as they can. But rest assured, we'll get everyone to their destination as quickly possible."

Molly and Maura welcomed the extra time in the Pavilion to chat with the friends they had made over the past few days. "Let's try to all get on the same bus," Molly said to her friends. "That way when we get there we'll all be together." Most of her new friends cheerfully agreed. Maura did the same with her friends, and when one of the 24 passenger "jeeps" arrived, they recognized the friendly driver Rudy and piled aboard. He skillfully drove the vehicle through the Monday morning rush-hour traffic in Sydney and soon was on the highway en route to Cape Breton University. As the rains and gusty winds continued, Rudy drove carefully until he reached Grand Lake Road. But rather than making an immediate left into CBU, he continued to follow Grand Lake Road and detoured into Glace Bay.

The young dancers, like schoolgirls everywhere, had segregated themselves by age groups. The oldest girls filled the rear seats of the bus with Molly and the youngest girls relegated to the front. The older girls were fascinated by their newest friend, Cara Patterson of Perth, Australia. Molly and her friends chatted with Avid Thomas from far off New Zealand. No one seemed to recognize or appreciate the short detour that their driver had made. After a short stop and a cellphone call, Rudy made one final turn into a gravel road, passing a sign which said 'Construction Zone-Hard Hats Required'. He then pulled into a graveled area next to several dark green trucks, each bearing a large logo of a white prancing horse on both sides, and bearing identification as 'Ingushetia Brothers Ltd. Restoration Specialists'. An automatic garage door opened and Rudy drove the bus into a well-lighted work area, lined with several wooden crates and boxes. A tall workman, but one wearing a 9mm sidearm entered the now open doors of the bus.

"Good morning young ladies," he began, "I do hope that my friend Mr. Rudolf Kadyrov has entertained you and treated you well during your brief journey here. My name is Mr. Ali Nuradilov, but you can call me Al, and I am the foreman here. Please remain seated on the bus as my friend Rudy drives us farther down the ramp to our parking area. And with the school bus door closed and Al still aboard, when they finally stopped they were well over a mile east and a hundred feet or more below the portal through which they entered the "parking garage."

"Now, the young ladies, I must ask you to leave the bus and sit on the benches that you will see on either side of the roadway. In case you are interested, you are in a former mine shaft known as "The Deeps" which is connected to the Miners Museum here at Glace Bay. Your parents will soon be notified of your location, and I can assure you that if you listen to the four young ladies who will soon join us, no harm at all will come to you. You may find that it's rather cool down here, but we have many overcoats and blankets that we will distribute to you to keep you nice and toasty warm. Our young ladies will show you to our bathroom facilities, and although they are a bit primitive, they are no worse than what you'd find at an outdoor festival. Ah, I can hear the young ladies coming now."

Rudy re-boarded the school bus and drove it several yards further into the mine. A few seconds later a four-wheel drive 'Gator off-road vehicle carrying two young women arrived on the scene, followed by a second vehicle about a minute later. All four women disembarked from the vehicles, both of which were carrying large cardboard boxes in its cargo area, "Allow me to introduce the young ladies who will be here with you today. This first young lady," he said pointing to the driver of the first vehicle, "is Ms. Fatima Dudaeva (Fay) and this is Maryam Vakhaeva (Mary). Mary is also a Registered Nurse, and will help you if you're feeling unwell."

Miss Vakhaeva, somewhat older than the others, spoke first. "Hi everyone," she said in perfect English. "I know you must be confused and perhaps a little upset about what's happening, but as I'm sure that Al has told you no harm will come with you, as long as you follow the directions that we give you. But to make things a little easier for all of you let me tell you what our English names are. I go by Mary, and my good friend here goes by Fay. The two women on the other truck go by Sandy and Kami. You'll soon get used to us and will try to be as helpful to you as we can under the circumstances. I know you all worried about soiling those beautiful dancing costumes, and I would be too." As she spoke her three companions opened the large cardboard containers which were strapped to the backs of the 'Gaters. "It's a tradition in our culture, just like in yours that we wear special clothing on special occasions. We call ours a "Chador," and I must admit that it is somewhat less decorative than your beautiful dresses. We have a selection of Chadors in these boxes, and I will ask each of you to put one on to cover your very attractive, and I would expect, costly, dancing dresses."

As she spoke her three companions handed out Chadors, gauging the size of each young girl in the group with a practiced eye. "Now you have two choices here," Mary continued. "You can either wear the Chador as sort of a cloak or a robe over your dress, or you can go back to the school bus and remove your dress and wear just the Chador. I would suggest to you though, that it's going to be reasonably cool in here; Al has reminded me that the temperature in here is about 55°F and hardly ever changes, and you may want all the warmth you can get. The Chadors we brought are winter ones, made of lambswool, and should keep you warm and comfortable. Later on, we'll go up front and bring back sleeping bags for everyone, and the men have prepared a sleeping room in one of the alcoves just off the main road. I understand that they have covered the sleeping area with about 2 inches of very fine straw to make it as comfortable as they can. And speaking of comfort, in another alcove just to our left you'll find eight'Porta Potties' for your further comfort.

The only thing that I ask you, indeed I require of you, is that you do not leave this area and go back up the road without one of us escorting you. But we believe that we've anticipated all of your needs, and there will be no reason for you to leave this immediate area. And, while I don't want to frighten you unnecessarily, anyone who does leave this area without permission will be in serious trouble, and we will deal with that trouble appropriately. So, my dear young ladies, I suggest that you make yourselves as comfortable as you can be, and clear your mind of worries. If you have any cell phones with you, I must tell you (even those of you who are on Canadian networks) that they will not work here in the coal mine. As Al may have told you, you are about 100 feet below the waters of the Atlantic Ocean at this point. The mine continues to a depth of about 300 feet below sea level if you were to go past the school bus. There is no reason for you to do that, and in fact, it may be dangerous to go much further than the bus. Now I'll be glad to ask any questions that you might have.

Annie Riley spoke up. "Who are you, why are we here, and how long do we have to put up with this crap?" She asked aggressively. Mary looked at her sternly.

"In our culture, we are taught to welcome guests graciously, and guests are expected to act graciously in return. Nevertheless, your questions deserve answers. While most of you, I am sure, are Irish, or of Irish descent, we are Chechen. And, just like Ireland throughout history, our small nation has been oppressed by colonial forces, in our case by Russia. And just like in Irish history, where six times in 300 years the people rose in revolt before striking for their freedom in 1916, so have our people. Thousand – many say hundreds of thousands – of our fellow countrymen have died in the struggle for freedom. All of us here are members of the 'Chechen diaspora'; our families came to North America many years ago. But just like in your families, our homeland burns in our hearts, and we do all we can to keep the message before the world that the Chechen people too have been downtrodden for the last two centuries."

"We will ask you to remain with us until that message is clear to everyone in the Western world and that Western political leaders agree to try our case before the World Court at the Hague, the United Nations and the rest of the world. We are all followers of Islam, and we mean you no harm. But we're going to have you remain with us until the message is clear that our daughters, our sisters, our elderly parents are as valuable as two dozen Irish folk dancers, and that our needs and desires for freedom must no longer be ignored. Now, if you would put on the Chadors which we provided to you, then Faye and Sandy will take the vehicles back to the portal where you entered to bring back supplies of food, water, and other necessities to make your stay as comfortable as we can."

CHAPTER ELEVEN: AS YOU WATCH THE YOUNG ONES GO

Erin and Pat waited patiently as all of the dancers boarded the buses and departed for CBU. After all had left, Erin and Pat lined up and, along with all of the other waiting parents boarded the remaining buses. The ride took longer than on previous days; traffic remains heavy in downtown Sydney, and the remnants of the accident on Grand Lake Road had just been moved to the side allowing traffic to pass.

They soon arrived at the Broadmore Playhouse, which, with the RBC Theatre, would host the semifinals rounds of the Oireachtas. "I sure hope that Maura and Molly were able to keep their dresses dry," Erin said to Pat. "While I don't think they'll have air-conditioning running on a day like today, I wouldn't want the kids to catch a cold with the weather like it is outside."

"I think they'll be okay, Erin. There were volunteers with large umbrellas when they boarded the bus, and there's a portico here as well as one at the RBC Theatre. I'm more concerned as to where they got off the bus. It has to be one of these two buildings though, I'm sure."

They entered the Broadmore Playhouse and looked around. The usual excitement and confusion which preceded any portion of an Oireachtas were evident, with the additional complication of several sets of parents looking for their daughters.

"I'll tell you what, Erin" Pat offered. "You go to the right, and I'll go to the left and the first one of us that finds either of the kids raise your hands and wave."

"Sounds like a plan," Erin replied. "And it's good that they don't have the air-conditioning running in here, there's enough cool air coming in through the lobby."

Both parents searched in vain for the next few minutes and regrouped by the door. "Well, that figures," Pat said to Erin. "They're probably over at the RBC Theatre. For any event as well organized as this was on the first couple days, toss in a little rain and a stiff breeze, and everything is turned upside down."

"Well Pat," Erin responded, "Fortunately it's not far from here to the RBC Theatre; let's go find a volunteer and explain the situation and borrow an umbrella." She did, and returned in a few minutes ready to brave the elements. Fortunately, the rain had slowed somewhat, and they made it to the theater without becoming any wetter.

Once again, they split up to search among the milling crowd of parents and dancers. When they returned to the front door, they were both dismayed that neither had seen either Molly or Maura. "Where can they be?" Erin asked. "I saw them get on the bus, and there are no other stops other than these two buildings. Should I go and check the restrooms?"

"Yeah, when don't you do that," Pat replied. "I'm going to try to find someone in charge and see if anyone knows what's happening. I'll meet you here if I don't spot you coming out of the ladies room."

Pat soon located a Ms. Chloe Dunne, whose name tag read 'Building Coordinator.' Several other parents were standing near her table. "Pardon me, but we're looking for our daughters who left on an earlier bus and can't seem to find them either here or at the Broadmore Playhouse. Do you have an idea where they might be? "

"No, I'm sorry that I don't. But several families are asking the same question about their dancers. Where they on a smaller bus? I think they carry about half as many students, er, I mean dancers, than the regular school buses."

"Yes, they were," he replied "are all of the other parents looking for dancers who had ridden that bus? If I recall correctly from yesterday, the driver was an amiable fellow named Rudy. I believe, but I'm not sure, that he may have been the driver again today."

Erin walked up behind him and overheard the conversation. It was clear from her demeanor at that her anxiety level was rising. "I didn't find them in the bathrooms, and I have no idea what's going on."

Ms. Dunne replied. "Let me call the program director and report what I'm hearing and see if she knows anything, and if she does not then, I will strongly recommend that she contact the Cape Breton Regional Police. I know there must be some logical explanation for this; I don't know what it might be. She dialed and spoke briefly with Ann Brennan, the General Manager of the Oireachtas who had just heard from the Building Coordinator at Broadmore with essentially the same issues. "Ms. Brennan is contacting the police right now, and if anything unfortunate has happened, they should know what it is. She suggests that all parents remain where they are, to avoid the danger of being injured or becoming ill from the weather. Sit tight. We are delaying the beginning of the semifinals until we find the location of our missing dancers."

Meanwhile, Sgt. Dan McCann and Constable Tommy Franks sat in their cruiser in the parking lot of the Swiss Chalet Restaurant just south of the Mayflower Mall. Sgt. McCann assisted the rookie constable in completing the paperwork resulting from the nearby road accident at Young Street and Grand Lake Road. They had barely begun the report when a call came across the police radio, reporting an 'incident' at Cape Breton University.

The dispatcher provided only the most basic information; people were upset because a small busload of participants at the Oireachtas had gone astray. Constable Franks picked up the microphone and inquired, "Can you describe the small bus please?" The dispatcher responded that it was a 24-passenger vehicle from the Cape Breton and Victoria School District, and it was last seen departing the Esplanade Street area at about 9:15 AM.

Constable Franks turned to Sgt. McCann. "You know, Sarge, I saw a bus matching that description pass through the intersection when I was on the traffic post. I wonder if that's the one they are looking for?"

"Well, we came South from Glace Bay, and I'll tell you there aren't too many places between here and the Uni where the bus could turn off. Let's responded to the call and head up to CBU."

They proceeded without lights or siren and allowing for the rain, wind, and traffic, crossed into the University in six minutes. "At what time did you see the bus passed you, Tommy?"

"It had to be after the accident and after the tow truck had cleared the vehicles, Sarge." I had 'Ocean View Towing' on the scene at 9:35, and they reported all clear at 9:48. So if the bus were moving at the speed of traffic, the latest it would have arrived at the Uni was, oh, five minutes before ten. We'll give them a break and say 10 o'clock Sarge. Does that make any sense to you?"

"Beats me, but why don't we do this before we go to the main admin building. Let's stop over at security, and ask them to do a fast-forward on the camera that covers their access driveway off Grand Lake Road.

It took only a few minutes with the tape to confirm that the bus hadn't entered the campus. They returned to their cruiser and drove to the administrative building, where they were redirected to the RBC Theatre.

Meanwhile, Lauren Burke and Ellie Collins of Feis Nova Scotia had escorted the distraught parents from the Broadmore Playhouse to the RBC Theatre and had arranged the use of a rehearsal room on the second floor for the parents of the now presumed-missing dancers. Sgt. McCann and Constable Franks joined them, and the place fell silent in their presence.

"We understand that the bus carrying your children has gone astray. Cape Breton Regional Police (CBRP) have received no reports of an accident involving the vehicle, and Constable Franks and I have just checked from Mayflower Mall to the University. We believe that we may have seen this bus on the highway between 9:35 and 9:50 this morning, about ninety minutes ago. CBRP are taking this very seriously and Staff Sgt. Morrison, Commander of Region Three, is en route to the University, and we have also notified our RCMP colleagues. I know you must be terribly concerned; I have two young daughters myself, and I can't imagine how terrible you must all feel at this moment. Please help us by remaining in this room for a few more minutes until Staff Sgt. Marie Morrison arrives, and she should be able to provide you with more information. And, one last request: The two young ladies from the organizing committee will ask you for the full names, ages, and hometowns of the young dancers on this bus. Now, please forgive me, while my partner and I assist in the area-wide search for the bus and its occupants."

The parents soon compiled the information requested:

24 PASSENGERS

Brennan, Rachel age 13 Atlanta GA

Macdonald, Cindy age 14 Chicago IL

Mackenna, Clodagh age 14 Boston MA

Brady, Emily age 12 Dallas TX

Clarke, Cindy age 11 Boston MA

Dunne, Annie age 13 Norfolk VA

Flaherty, Ellie age 13 Toronto ON

Flyn, Mia age 13 Reno NV

Hayes, Alice age 12 Dallas TX

Leary, Eve age 11 San Marcus TX

Lincoln, Molly age 11 New City NY

Lincoln, Maura age 13 New City NY

Maguire, Chloe age 11 Chicago IL

Mccarthy, Maura age 13 Calgary AB

Mcgraw, Maggie age 11 Columbus OH

Moore, Cindy age 12 South Bend IN

Moran, Sophie age 12 Denver CO

Murphy, Ciara age 14 York PA

Nolan, Ellie age 12 Hartford CT

O'Farrell, Olivia age 11 Ft.Worth TX

O'Mahony, Laura age 13 Cincinnati OH

Patterson, Cora age17 Perth WA, AUST.

Riley, Annie age 13 York PA

Thomas, Avid age 16 Wellington NZ

White, Sadie age 14 Calgary AB

After leaving the Monday morning command staff weekly meeting as quickly as she could, Staff Sgt. Marie Morrison prepared to drive to CBU. On the way out of the CBRP building she was stopped by the superintendent's secretary. "You have an urgent phone call from RCMP Inspector Owen Pelletier. He asks that you return the call as soon as possible." She thanked the secretary and asked to use her telephone. She dialed the RCMP barracks on Victoria Road, and Inspector Pelletier came to the phone within a few seconds.

"You've heard about the missing bus load of kids out at the dance competition at the University?" Inspector Pelletier asked.

"I have indeed Inspector, and I'm on my way out there right now. Do you have any new information for me?"

"I'm afraid I do; Are you at a secure place where you can speak?" "I'm still at our headquarters, Inspector. Go on."

"Okay. Canadian Coast Guard Radio Station VCO in Sydney has received a number of strange radio transmissions beginning about 10:45 this morning and repeating every five minutes. After receiving the first one, they attempted to direction-find the source of the second signal, and it appeared to be coming from somewhere around Albert Bridge. They tried it with the third transmission as well and it seems to be coming from somewhere in the Highlands National Park. And the last one which was received about 11:20 AM and seems to be due South along HY-104. That in itself is interesting, but you had better come over and picked me up and I will show you the transcript of the message as received. Clearly, since all of this is happening on VHF channel 24, it's either a mobile station or a series of vehicles transmitting the same message sequentially. How soon can you get over here to pick me up and we can ride together to the University?"

"I'll be there in ten and then we can hightail it up to CBU. One of my sergeants and a constable were there earlier, but have returned to aid in the search. I can get them back to the University in a few minutes if you think that's advisable."

"Yes, do that, and I think you ought to notify your Victims Assistance Unit to proceed to the Uni as well, but ask them not to enter the room where the families are waiting until we get there. This is about as serious, Marie, as anything you and I have ever seen." "I'm leaving here now Inspector."

When he entered the patrol car, Pelletier handed SSgt Morrison the transcription. She read it silently:

MANIFESTO OF THE CHECHEN BROTHERHOOD IN EXILE

For centuries, we the Chechen people have been the victims of imperialist Russia's wrath. For centuries Canada and the international community has ignored our agony, our basic human rights and our struggle to be free. For the past decade both Muslim and Western leaders have remained silent. Now, disturbed by the latest revelation of Russian war crimes, they are calling in vain for an investigation of the summary execution, rape and looting by Russian troops in our beloved homeland.

Your own CBC has recently broadcast footage of Russian soldiers piling mutilated Chechen bodies into a mass grave.

This is but the tip of a huge iceberg of Russian atrocities in Chechnya. Since the beginning of the invasion, observers have reported that Russian forces have violated all norms of warfare and international conventions, using massive firepower against civilians everywhere. Recently, Russian missiles killed 140 and wounded 400 civilians at a market place, a hospital and other areas of the our capital, Grozny.

Furthermore, Chechen males from the ages of 10 to 70 are swept into concentration camps and many such men detained at Russian checkpoints have disappeared.

Yet Canada and other international governments are not matching their words of criticism with action.

The Canadian government welcomed Russian assurances that war criminals would be handed over to military prosecutors for investigation. That is no better than asking rapists and thugs to be their own judges.

Most disturbingly, Christian and Muslim voices have remained as mute as ever. We must not forget that Russia remains a last bastion of colonial imperialism in the current post-colonial world. Russia invaded Chechnya in 1859 and has since killed tens of thousands of Chechens every time we have demanded freedom.

We declared independence from Russia in 1991 when the other former Soviet republics broke with Russia. The West swiftly recognized the Baltic republics (Estonia, Latvia, and Lithuania) but mysteriously ignored the call of Chechnya to be free. Heeding the West's warning, Russia did not invade the Baltic States. But Chechnya was abandoned.

Like the peoples of Estonia, Latvia, Lithuania, the Chechens deserve to be free. It is unfair and unethical for humanity to support the freedom of all these peoples and ignore that of the Chechens.

We have taken these young women hostage. They are clothed in the folk dress of your own people. Are their lives more valuable than those of our own sisters and daughters? We wish them no harm, but if they must die so that the plight of thousands of our own children is clear to the world, let their blood be on your heads!

You will receive further instructions shortly. If you make any attempt to attack us, at the first shot these beautiful, precious children will die instantly. Allah Akbar! Chechnya lives!

THE MINERS' MUSEUM, GLACE BAY NS

CHAPTER 12: I'VE BEEN DOWN UNDERGROUND

While the police were concerned about the safety and welfare of the parents of the twenty-four hostages, the dancers themselves were concerned primarily with each other. Little Cindy Clarke of Boston had only just turned 11 and was having a hard time coping with the situation in which she found herself. Crying inconsolably, she was comforted by the only Australian among the group of hostages, Cora Patterson who was almost 18. Most of the other young hostages were in a state of mild shock.

Fatima Dudaeva (Fay), herself a native of Cape Breton who grew up near the Canso Straits, offered whatever reassurance she could that no harm would befall the children. She was unaware, though, of the wording of the manifesto being transmitted to the outside world. "I've good news for you," she said. "How many of you like pizza?" Almost all of the girls raised their hands. "Well, Kammie Sheripova is on her way to pick up six large pizzas and several bottles of soft drinks for your lunch today. And we've arranged with others to make a hot dinner for each of you every day that you are with us." As soon as those words left her mouth, she realized that she might have further frightened the young dancers. "Not that I think you're going to be here with us very long at all, but you can be sure that you'll have good nutritious meals and that your health will not suffer unnecessarily."

"But tell me,are there any of you who are dependent on upon medicine each day?" Two girls, Cindy Moore, age 12, of South Bend Indiana and Ellie Nolan, also age 12 of Hartford Connecticut, raise their hands. Nurse Maryam Vakhaeva (Mary) spoke to each privately. "Hello, Cindy, it's good to meet you, although perhaps it would be better under different circumstances. Can you tell me a little bit about your health issues?"

"The girl stammered and then disclosed that she had asthma, which would be irritated by any stress. "The coal dust in this disused mine probably won't help either," the nurse thought to herself. The girl continued that she relied heavily on a rescue inhaler. She reached into the pocket of the Chador and pulled out her red ProAir HFA personal breathing aid. "This is the kind that I usually use, and it's about half full now. My mom won't let me leave the house without this in my pocket." The nurse nodded and went on to the other young girl.

"How about you Ellie," she asked gently. The youngster replied. "I am a person with type I diabetes and I don't have my insulin with me. My mom had it in her purse when we got separated at the cruise ship pavilion."

"When is your next dose due, Cindy?"

"Well, I check my sugars routinely throughout the day,

ma'am. In fact, I should be checking right now. But I usually inject the insulin about 30 minutes before mealtime. I don't think I'll be able to eat the pizza when it comes. Please, can you help me?"

"I certainly will, Cindy and if necessary will get you out of here within the next hour or so. Hang in there, child, and we will do whatever we can."

Nurse Mary went to the small alcove to the right of the tunnel road where a field telephone had been placed by the "freedom fighters" as they prepared for the hostages. She rang the group at the access portal and spoke urgently with Ali Nuradilov. "We've got a real problem down here, Al," she said. "We have a brittle type I diabetic, aged 12, here who is insulin dependent, and her mother has her insulin in her purse. We have to take care of the situation immediately, Ali."

Al thought for a long moment and then replied. "Okay, here's what we're going to do. Get her on one of the 'Gators and send her up front. Then I'll have one of the brothers here drive her over to the Glace Bay General Hospital. We'll use one of our vehicles from here to save time. You stay back there with the other girls, and I'll send Sandy right down to get her. Be as quiet about this as you can, though, so that we don't disturb or raise false hopes unnecessarily among the others."

Ellie was transported to the portal within a few minutes, and Ilyas Tchermoeff, at 18, the youngest member of the Chechen Brotherhood involved in the operation, volunteered to drive her to Glace Bay General. Once she was in the vehicle, he asked her to remove the Chador and to leave it in the back of the panel truck. "Please don't be scared, Ellie. I have a little sister about your age back in Toronto. But, this is what we're going to do, Ellie. I'm going to drop you off at the hospital, and I will get a wheelchair, and I will ask you to sit in it for about five minutes until I'm able to leave the hospital grounds. You understand that if you don't follow these instructions you are putting my life, the life of my comrades and most importantly the life of your fellow dancers at risk. Do you promise to do as I asked? Ellie, on the verge of hypoglycemia, just nodded affirmatively.

As soon as the vehicle had left the parking area, Ali picked up a handheld radio and contacted the brothers who were manning observations post in the attic of a cottage in the Miner's Village, and the museum's tower. Speaking Chechen, he informed them of developments. While he had anticipated at least 24 to 36 hours before discovery to allow the situation to stabilize, nevertheless as an experienced freedom fighter in Bosnia-Herzegovina and Chechnya for the past 15 years, he knew that operations rarely evolved the way they were planned. "Be very aware and observant. We've had to send a little girl for medical care unexpectedly. I'm certain that within the hour the police will know where we are holding the hostages. What they don't know now, but will shortly learn is that we have 120 pounds of gelignite and C4 explosives distributed around the tunnel. If they make any move into our area, we will detonate them and flood the tunnels with millions of gallons of seawater immediately. Allah Akbar!"

Within the hour, the Victim Support Unit had arrived at the University and was briefed by Staff Sgt. Morrison. At the firm suggestion of the RCMP command, they did not inform the VSU of the content of the Chechen Manifesto. The team, led by Detective Constable Arrha Srinivasan met with the families of the missing girls and provided as much information as they could about the progress of the search. Meanwhile Staff Sgt. Morrison and Inspector Pelletier returned to CBU's administration building and met with the facilities director, who made the MacDonald Arena available for the joint police agency's incident room and command center. Within another hour the large mobile communications trucks of both the RCMP and CBRP parked adjacent to the arena and were immediately available for secure communications and access to any radio frequency 'from dirt to daylight.'

Both Morrison and Pelletier had briefed their senior officers of the current status, and their assessment of the

threat to the hostages by the Chechen Brotherhood.
RCMP Deputy Commissioner Arthur Rutherford and
CBRP Commissioner Samuel Paisley both arrived on
scene shortly after noon and took full operational
command of the police response to the incident. After
being briefed on the latest developments, both senior
officers visited the families in the rehearsal hall. DC
Rutherford, in his full red Mounted Police Dress
Uniform, spoke first.

"Let me begin by offering my apologies for letting this
happen on our watch. We were devastated to learn of the
hijacking – and that's the best word that I can think to use
– of the school bus and the 24 children aboard. The entire
RCMP Nova Scotia command has been put on Red Alert,
and we are bringing additional constables to this area
from throughout the province immediately. We have
learned within the last few minutes that this hijacking
and kidnapping seems to be politically motivated, and
the RCMP Regional Terrorism Squad is en route here
from Halifax. They should be here within the next ninety
minutes or so. Now let me turn the microphone over to
Sam Paisley, the Commissioner of the Cape Breton
Regional Police."

"I too offer my most abject apologies that this happened
in Cape Breton. I am a native Cape Bretoner, and I am
personally offended that any group of terrorists would be

so bold as to attack anyone here in what is essentially my hometown. I know that in the world in which we now live it can happen anywhere, but I myself live here in Glace Bay, as have my forefathers for five generations." Staff Sgt. Morrison stepped forward and silently slipped a single sheet of paper on the podium. The Commissioner glanced at it and continued. "We've established a timeline indicating that the bus left the cruise pavilion at about 9:33 AM, and was spotted passing through an accident zone at Grand Lake and Young Street, 6 miles south of here, at 9:47 AM. Given the weather and traffic, it should have entered CBU at 9:53, and the first reports of its non-arrival here at the University were made by you, the parents shortly after 10 AM.

We've mapped concentric circles based upon the maximum distance the vehicle could have driven during that time and are concentrating our resources within those circles." As he was speaking, Ssgt. Morrison brought forward another sheet of paper. "We've just learned from the staff at Glace Bay General Hospital, that a 12-year-old girl had just been admitted to the accident ward, suffering from what appeared to be insulin deficiency." Ellie Nolan's parents gasped. "To the best of our knowledge she is going to be fine; the staff at the General Hospital has stabilized her condition. More importantly, she has provided valuable information as to the possible location where the hostages are being held. Both CBRP and RCMP officers are in route to that area now, and we will provide additional information to you shortly. Mr. and Mrs. Nolan, if you are ready, I've just been informed that two constables are waiting outside the door ready to drive you the short distance to the hospital."

He continued. "And now, with the understanding that the total amount of information available at this moment is quite limited, and there are some things that we are not able to disclose, so as not to jeopardize the ongoing search and investigation, I'll be happy to answer whatever questions you may have."

The mother of Eve Leary raised her hand. "I just saw a post on Twitter saying that you have had a detailed message from the terrorists. Is that true, and what can you tell us about what they said?"

The Commissioner paused for a moment. "Let me refer that question to my colleague from the RCMP. DC Rutherford?"

The Mountie approached the microphone. "I must caution you the social media is already rampant with idle speculation from those who claim knowledge which they do not have. But to answer your question frankly and honestly, yes we have. Shortly after we learned that the bus had been hijacked, our colleagues in the Canadian Coast Guard began receiving a repeated message on one of the ship to shore channels from those who purport to hold your daughters hostage. It was not signed, but we believe that because of the timing it is connected with their disappearance."

Jim Brady of Dallas, whose daughter Emily had been on the school bus, jumped up with an additional question. "The Coast Guard? Does that mean that you think that they have been placed on a boat of some kind? Should we be concerned about the cruise ship and their crew that you provided as housing for the dance competition? What are we to make of this?"

"No, we do not believe that there is any connection with any boat or ship at all. As I mentioned, the message was repeated several times, but the Coast Guard quickly instituted direction finding, and they traced the messages to three separate locations, all of which are well inland and not connected to any boat at all. They estimate that at least three vehicles, equipped with VHF ship to shore radios were "roving" around the highways of Cape Breton."

"Incidentally, within the last five minutes, I have been informed that the doctors in the accident ward at Cape Breton General learned from young Ellie that she believes that they were being held in a coal mine and that the trip from the mine to the hospital took just a few minutes. She also gave us a very detailed idea description of the vehicle and driver. You can appreciate that I cannot disclose that particular information to you at this moment, but the All Points Bulletin which we and the CBPD jointly released has made that information available to all of our constables."

Several other family members rose to ask what were essentially redundant questions, or questions which the police were not in a position to reveal. Finally, the Deputy Commissioner said, "We will leave you now with our support unit, but I promise you sincerely and without reservation that the moment I receive any significant information, I will pass it on to you. God bless you, God bless your young daughters – and God bless Cape Breton."

'MARY' 'KAMMIE' 'KATHY'

CHAPTER THIRTEEN: THE CAPTAIN CALLS – I MUST OBEY

After the twenty-three remaining hostages had devoured their pizzas, nurse Mary announced that because of the young dancer's medical condition, they had released Ellie Nolan to travel to the regional hospital in Glace Bay. The remaining dancers busied themselves in preparing the sleeping bags and other materials which had been brought from the portal in anticipation of at least a single overnight stay. Concurrently, Ali Nuradilov made a tape recording to be aired directly from the portal area of the mine. "There is no need now to carry out the mobile transmissions. If they don't know where we are now they certainly will learn from the young lady we had to release to the hospital" he said to his companions.

The tape began:

ATTENTION CAPE BRETON POLICE!

"This message is from the Chechen Brotherhood striking for the freedom of the oppressed nation of Chechnya. We are now in possession of the Miners Museum and Miners Village in Glace Bay, Nova Scotia. We are well armed, and our young guests are well treated.

We hereby declare that the one square mile bounded by Birkley Street to the south, Blackett Street to the north, Museum Street to the west, and 1000 meters offshore of

Museum Point are now considered sovereign Chechnya territory.

Any attempt of any person to enter this square mile will be met with force of arms, and their immediate death at the hands of the Chechen Brotherhood. Furthermore, we warn you that we have 120 pounds of gelignite and C4 explosives distributed around the mine tunnel. If you make any move into our area, we will detonate these powerful explosives and flood the tunnels with million of gallons of seawater resulting in the deaths of these young women.

These twenty-three remaining hostages are being held as a guarantee of action by the governments of the West and of the Islamic world in bringing the long-standing grievances of Chechnya and her people to the World Court Of Justice at The Hague and to the United Nations in New York.

Please, we entreat you, if you wish to see these beautiful children alive once more do not enter the one square mile which I have described. If you do so, you do at your own risk and in peril to the life of our guests."

He repeated the message for the next thirty minutes on channel 24 of the Marine VHF radio bands.

Meanwhile, after exchanging a few words with several of the families in the rehearsal hall, both Rutherford and

Paisley returned to the incident room and command center at MacDonald Arena. In their absence, several teams of constables from each agency had been drafted to assist in the investigation. Shortly after they arrived, the RCMP communications van signaled them that a message was being transmitted from the Chechen Brotherhood. They listened attentively to the transmission directly from the Miners Museum.

"Several hundred pounds of gelignite and C-4? These perps are not fooling around" commented Commissioner Paisley.

"Where is this Miners Museum that he's talking about?" questioned Deputy Commissioner Rutherford. "Is it here in Glace Bay and what do we know about it?"

Paisley signaled to all of his men to assemble at the newly erected whiteboard. "How many of you have ever been to the Miners Museum?" Every constable raised his hand. "Good, very good, what do you know about the construction of the building?"

No one responded immediately. "Come on; you must know something if you were there. What's the building like?"

Sgt. McCann spoke up. "Well truthfully Sir, I suspect that most of us were there as little kids on school field trips," Rutherford muttered under his breath. "Well is there anyone here that knows anything about the place, other than where to get a free ice cream cone when you're on your school outings? Come on; we can do better than that."

McCann continued. "I know a fellow who used to be the manager there, back when it was all volunteers. I can give him a call if you like and we can send a patrol car to pick him up and bring him here. The last I heard, he lived in Caledonia, not 15 minutes away from here."

"Make it so, Sergeant."

Mr. Tom Callahan arrived in the patrol car a few minutes later. Both Paisley and Rutherford greeted him and escorted him farther into the incident room. "As you may know, Mr. Callahan, the building has been seized by terrorists of the Chechen Brotherhood. How could that have happened?"

"Well, the museum has been closed since mid-June for emergency repairs and much-needed renovations. The winters of the past forty years have not been kind to the building, and the last time the engineers inspected the building they told us that there were dangerous conditions, particularly in the roof and exterior walls, which needed to be addressed before we could reopen the building to paying customers. We petitioned the CB regional council for a grant and went out with competitive bids. A company named Ingushetia Brother's Restorations from Pictou County came in with the lowest bid. They're due to finish the restoration work sometime around 15 August. While we did lose a critical part of our "season," the alternative of causing serious injury to someone was too great to ignore."

"That's all very well Mr. Callahan, but what we're interested in now is the mine tour which you offer to your visitors. Where exactly does that go?"

Well, sir, we don't advertise it as a 'mine tour'; we advertise it as an 'underground experience.' The museum was built adjacent to an entrance portal to the old Imperial Coal Company, Shaft 19. We use only the first, oh, 450 feet or so, and have decorated the area as best we could to resemble how the underground workings might appear. And since all of us volunteers had worked in the mines for years, we had a pretty good idea of what people would expect. We sloped the floor and the roof and when the lights were extinguished, well, with the rough walls and the roughly two tons of coal which we embedded in the walls and spread around the floors, the average visitor couldn't tell the difference. We could, of course, but we promised each other we wouldn't do anything to give away the magic. It was kind of like something Disney would do, come to think about it."

"Well then, where is the 'underground experience,'

relative to the Imperial Coal Company's shaft?"

"Oh, for much of the way they are parallel to each other. Only about three feet separate the "simulated" mine shaft and the real thing. The Imperial shaft begins at the far end of the simulation and then drops into the workings. That shaft was one of the longer mine tunnels constructed by Imperial, and it runs about 2 miles out under what is now called Museum Point into the open waters of the bay."

"How difficult would it be for someone to break through the wall at the end of the simulation?"

Mr. Callahan thought for a moment. "Not difficult at all; the actual rear wall of the simulator is composed of drywall and plywood, supported by regular two by fours. You could remove that entire wall in, oh maybe half an hour or so, and you would be in the Imperial Company's original shaft. In fact, I had been in that shaft several times when we were constructing the "experience."

There is also a second entrance, directly into Imperial's Shaft 19, and we used that during construction to access the back of the property. There is an open work area, that once was the changing room for the miner's showers, and a very long and gently dropping roadway back to the working face. While I don't have the numbers before me,

I'd estimate that once you enter that portal, you're about 1/2 mile to the point where you go underwater, and within another half-mile or so you'd be about 300 feet below the low tide point in the bay.

In those days, before mining regulations became so restrictive, you only needed about 100 feet of overburden for the mine to be considered safe. Now of course, if you were to open a mine similar to these nineteenth-century workings, you would need at least 700 feet of overburden beneath the seabed. But the interesting thing about that shaft is that the roof of the roadway is almost completely coal, as is the roadway where the mine bogeys used to run. And, although it's fairly narrow for a working mine, in those days before mechanization, it was plenty wide for a team of ponies to pull the carts and still have room to pass each other coming and going."

The senior police officers thanked Mr. Callahan for his information, and before he left, they asked him if he knew of any detailed maps or diagrams of the Imperial Coal Company's workings in the area. "I don't have any," he said, "but I'm sure they exist somewhere, perhaps over at the Department of Natural Resources' field office in Glace Bay. If your constables would like to stop there before they take me back home, I could ask them to dig out the appropriate sheets for you." Again they thanked him for his time and his assistance.

A few minutes after he and the constables left, there was a loud disturbance outside the MacDonald Arena. Two SUVs, with lights flashing roared up to the building.

"God help us all," thought Commissioner Paisley, "the 'snake eaters' have arrived."

His guess was correct. Within the minute, six burly members of the RCMP Anti-Terrorism Squad barged into the incident room. Led by Chief Superintendent Harry Wilson, they stood at attention in the presence of DC Rutherford. "What help do you need, Deputy Commissioner? We have stayed in contact with Halifax all the way up here, and we have a fair idea as to what you are facing. We also have additional equipment coming behind us, including a semi-trailer with two of our Bearcat assault vehicles primed and ready to go. Where would you like us to be, sir?"

"Well, for the time being, we want you to hang on until we have a better idea of the circumstances. We have an unknown number of actors who are threatening the lives of the hostages, and we just had a briefing from a gentleman who is at least familiar with the building where they are being held. We need to get more information before we make a move."

"The terrorist group has dared to declare a square mile of territory in Glace Bay as being part of the Chechnya

Republic, or whatever the hell they're calling their terrorist movement. I suspect that we will wait at least until darkness before we ask anyone to enter that area on a reconnaissance patrol. And to say that they are armed and dangerous would be a tremendous understatement. They claim to have explosives, they are no doubt heavily armed, and they threaten to kill any officer who enters that square-mile. Just stayed put for a moment, until we get a better handle on what's going on."

'You're not going to believe this, Boss," interjected Inspector Pelletier, "But we just called Pictou, and they have no record of this so-called 'Ingushetia Brother's Restorations" outfit. But according to one of the communications guys in the van, *Ingushetia* is the ancient name for Chechnya.

"Give me strength" was his only reply.

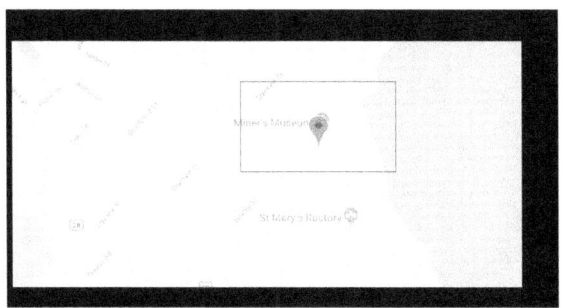

CHECHEN'S "NO-GO" AREA

IMPERIAL COAL COMPANY SHAFT 19

CHAPTER FOURTEEN: IN THE DARK RECESS OF THE MINES

After the pizza party, the girls sat around the dimly lit tunnel and tried to make sense of their situation. Alice Hayes, age 12 of Dallas shyly raised her hand with a question.

"There's no need to raise your hand, Alice. I know it's hard to believe, but you are among friends here" replied Kammie Khizrieva, who at age 26 was one of the youngest of the 'Guardian Angels' looking after the girls in the dark recesses of the mine. "What would you like to know Alice?" she continued.

"Well, you seem to know a lot about Ireland, but I don't know anything about Chechnya. I'm not even sure I pronounce it right, and I don't have any idea where it is. Can you tell us something about Chechnya?"

"Yes, of course, I can." replied Kami, who in her "other life" was a fourth-grade teacher in rural Manitoba. "Let me see. First of all it's a lovely place. There are mountains, lakes, fast running streams full of fish, and in the springtime and summer there are flowers everywhere.

My grandparents came to Canada back about 1917, when the Russian government which had always oppressed our people because of our Islamic faith, began a

crackdown on everyone living in the capital city of
Grozny. It was tough for them to leave our native land;
the history of Chechnya stretches all the way back to
about 8000 years ago, and we are, after all, the people
who are regarded as the first Caucasians. You probably
know that word in the context of Caucasians, Hispanics,
and African-Americans, but we are really the first
Caucasians – the people of the Caucasus. Just like you
sing songs about Ireland, and some of them are very sad,
especially when you sing about the famine and the
revolts and revolutions that plagued Ireland for so many
years, well, we ourelves sing songs too.

I think that Kathy Yandarbiyeva packed her old
boombox along when we came to help our fathers and
brothers. Let me see if I can talk her into letting us use it
for a little while. It may well be the last boombox ever
sold in North America; she once told me that she found it
on the closeout aisle at a discount store, but I know that
she has some of our songs on CDs."

She talked to Kathy, who loaned her the boombox, and
she returned and played several lovely tunes for the girls.
She saved her favorite for last and played 'Shaltak's Song'
which the people of Chechnya consider their national
anthem. The song, of course, was in Chechen, but Kami
sang along softly, and after the girls listen to her singing
she offered this translation:

No matter how unfair the wildfire of injustice in Chechnya,

You kept falling and rising again.

The lightning of Caucasus, the cradle of liberty,

Your honor was kept by your proud people.

The peace between your peoples is priceless wealth!

There is no other motherland for the Chechens.

Our lives and our deaths in the heart of our homeland,

We beg you to bless.

The ancestors' souls descend to Bashlam's peak.

The wave of Argun speaks our mother tongue.

Our lives blessed us with a great gift — you!

Shatlak's song gave us strength!

Love for work and courage, respect for all peoples,

Let this be pleasant news for you.

The Guardian of freedom, who has found its path

Live for us, oh worthy Chechnya

"And now I can tell you about another special treat that we are going to have this evening. After all, no one can live on pizza alone, so we have asked several of our friends who are not here with us in the mine if they wouldn't mind making a special Chechen dinner for all of us. When I was out getting the pizzas earlier, I stopped off at one of their homes and brought the food back here for our dinner. The men at the portal volunteered to warm it up for us at dinnertime – in return for a couple of platefuls for themselves, no doubt! They will use the kitchen of the restaurant in the museum to warm it up for us. We'll eat about 5:00 PM or so, I should think. But tell me this; do any of you drink tea?"

The young women from Australian and New Zealand were the first to raise their hands; indeed they waved them back and forth vigorously. About two-thirds of the young Canadian dancers also raise their hands and even a few of the Americans.

"Well you have to try it, it's good!" continue Kami, "we'll have some with dinner, and I'll teach you how to drink it the 'Chechen way'. But first let me tell you what the good mothers of our community have prepared for us today:

"For starters, they've made a dish from vine leaves stuffed with cheese. I'm sorry, but even though my mom made it for us at home, I can't remember the Chechen name.Then there's *Sorpa,* a somewhat spicy meat soup made with fried meat (lamb or beef), grilled vegetables (potatoes, onions, carrots, tomatoes and peppers), and herbs and often chickpea. That's my dad's favorite, especially when he's been out working with the cows on a snowy day.

The main course will be *Khinkli* – dumplings stuffed with diced lamb and smothered with *Satsvi,* that's walnut sauce. There's also *Lavash,* an unleavened soft flatbread that we as a scoop to get the last drop of that beautiful walnut sauce. And finally, for dessert, *Halva,* my favorite! It's crumbly and made from *Tahini* (sesame paste) or sunflower seed butter. The primary ingredients are nut butter and sugar."

After the hot dinner was served the dancers chatted among themselves, mostly about Feiseanna they had attended, or Feiseanna they hoped to participate in until Kami indicated that bedtime was near.

"All right, young ladies, I think it's time to get ready for bed. We have that alcove off to the left-hand side of the tunnel prepared as a sleeping area. There are several inches of fresh straw on the ground, and we have sleeping bags for everyone. Sandy thought to bring a small battery operated lantern to use as a night-light!

So perhaps now you'd all like to attend to your hygiene before going off to bed. We have four basins of water outside the alcove where the PortaPotties are set up, and we have a box of brand-new toothbrushes and several kinds of toothpaste, so take your pick. We also have, ahem! Those feminine products which all of us need at one time or another. I wished that I had been at the pharmacy when we sent the men to pick those up! They probably covered their faces and looked the other way."

"I have another suggestion for bedtime; why don't you sleep in pairs of two? You might want to have someone from your hometown, or a special friend close, to be with you during the night. As I say, we have plenty of sleeping bags for everyone, and you should be very comfortable, I should think. But if you need anything, we will take turns and at least one of us and be awake at all times throughout the night. As best we can, we'll do everything possible to make you comfortable. And don't forget your 'big sisters,' Cora and Avid, who have come from 16,000 km away just to dance here in Cape Breton, will always be with you in the room and I'm sure will help you if you need them".

After attending to their hygiene as directed, the girls turned in for the night. Molly and Maura, being the only sisters in the group, stayed close together. But there was one small item to address.

Since one of the original twenty-four dancers had left them, that reduction meant that someone would not have a partner. That person, not surprisingly, was Annie Riley. She looked first aloof and then dejected when she realized that no one wanted to partner with her. Maura said to Molly "I'm going to invite her to come over here and be with us. I realize that not too many people like her, and I don't really care for her myself, but we can't let her be all alone tonight after everything that happened today," Molly nodded. Maura left her to guard the sleeping bags and went up to the front of the alcove where Annie Riley was sitting alone. "Why don't you come back and be with my sister and me," Maura asked.

"I thought Kami said we should go two-by-two. I don't want to get into any trouble, or at least any more trouble than we're already in."

"Well if you can figure out a way to divide 23 by 2 and come up with 12 pairs, let me know. But my sister and I have a nice quiet spot in the back corner, and even if someone knew there were three rather than two of us there, I don't think anyone really would care."

Annie agreed and followed Maura back to the far left corner of the sleeping alcove. Maura had been correct; it was out of the direct line of sight from the entrance to the alcove, and it was about as private space as anyone could find given the circumstances.

"Go ahead and set your sleeping bag wherever you want," said Molly. Annie Riley chose the space directly in the corner so that she could talk to both Maura and Molly without having to turn around.

" You guys are nice, you know? You're both from the mid-Atlantic region, aren't you? I'm from York Pa. I was the first alternate in the U-14 age group, and got to come along when that other girl couldn't come because her mom got sick."

"Yeah. I heard your mom yelling at one of the volunteers about having to ride on the school buses. Boy, was she right!" whispered Molly.

"My mom is right about everything, or so she thinks. And she likes to get her own way too. We haven't got a lot of money, and my mom is always on my case to work harder at the dancing so that one day I can get a fancy job and we can get rich. How is your mom about dancing?"

"Well, she always says that we should keep dancing until it stops being fun. Then we can go off and do something else. But she danced competitively until she was nearly twenty, and both of us enjoy it so much that we wouldn't want to stop dancing now. In fact, there are lots of times around the house when we break into a jig or hornpipe, and mom watches it and laughs," said Maura.

"My mom doesn't laugh about much at all anymore. When she found out that it would cost $600 each way for her and me to fly up here, she figured we could save a couple of bucks by driving up here in our beat up old Subaru. I thought the car was going to break down about a half dozen times on the way, and each time it stalled mom got madder and madder. One time, once we got into Canada, mom must have spent twenty minutes on the side of the road, mentally converting liters into gallons and then another ten minutes converting Canadian dollars in US dollars, before she found the cheapest place to stop to refuel. We were running on fumes when we got there, and then she started yelling at the poor kid who was pumping the gas to make sure he didn't spill any.""So your mom is tough on you about dancing?" Molly asked.

Annie fell silent for a long moment. "She carries a big handbag everywhere she goes, and in that handbag, there's always an old wooden hairbrush. Anytime I'm slacking off at our dance academy, and she finds out about it, all she has to do is lift the handle out of the bag so that I can see it. And I know what that means. She's going to be so angry that I missed the semi-finals today that I'll probably get it good when I finally get home."

"But it's not our fault! Those gangsters stole our bus and are holding us against our will," said Molly. "How can she say it's your fault?"

"Everything's my fault, Molly. Everything," she whispered sadly.

"What about your dad?" Maura asked. "How does he feel

about all this?"

"I never had a dad," Annie Riley replied, sadly. "Well I mean, yes I did, but I don't know who he is or where he is now and I don't care. But if there's one thing that'll cause my mom to go completely crazy, it's asking anything about him. I tried that once, and I couldn't sit down for a couple of days."

"Well," Maura said, "we better get to sleep because we don't have any idea what tomorrow will bring. If you look at all the food and all the supplies that they have brought in here for us, I don't think the Chechens think we're going to be going home anytime soon. We just have to play it like it is and hope for the best. Molly and I are going to say our prayers now, and you can join in with us if you like." And after the bedtime prayers, the three girls tossed and turned for a while until they fell into an exhausted, yet uneasy night's sleep.

CHAPTER FIFTEEN: THE MAN WITH A TORCH IN HIS CAP

Monday, 8 August

Much had happened, but nothing changed really, in the week since the dancers had been hijacked. After a brief hiatus, the Oireachtas had continued and wrapped up on Wednesday as planned. The parents and dancers not directly involved departed for home and MV TORSHAVN sailed away to resume cruising in North American waters. The parents of the hostages were graciously offered free accommodations in the residence halls at CBU 'for the duration' and prayers were offered in churches throughout the region.

The media frenzy of the previous week faded somewhat, but the major news networks, always hungry for stories, continued to point their long-range cameras into the museum complex and interviewed anyone who professed to have any experience in underseas mining. Pundits pontificated, and reporters reported, breathlessly, that there was nothing to report.

The RCMP terrorist squad had infiltrated the compound in the dark of the moon on Friday but became alarmed when they saw several red laser dots appear on their uniforms, indicating they were within the gun-sights of the Chechens in the museum's sandbagged tower high above. They performed a strategic retreat and did not return to the compound. Ali and his comrades continued to make periodic appeals for the support of the western nations with little impact, although Australia and New Zealand promised to champion the matter on the international stage.

In addition, the Canadian Coast Guard, which had been tremendously helpful during the entire event, dispatched a 279-foot high endurance vessel, CCGS George Andrews to patrol offshore. This was intended to prevent any ships from entering the exclusion zone and triggering a tragedy, but also to covertly deploy highly directional hydrophones, scanning the area for any sound it could detect from the subsurface mine.

And Constable Tommy Franks, who had worked twelve-hour shifts in the incident room continuously since the hijacking a week ago, went home once again to his wife Amanda and his five-year-old son Joey.

Arriving home, he kissed his wife and son as always and reached into the refrigerator for a beer. "How's it going, Tommy?" Amanda asked.

"Same-old same-old" Tommy replied. "It's like a circus without a ringmaster in there. They have me researching everything under the sun and, to be honest I would be delighted if someone relieved me from duty in the incident room and let me get back to my nice battered old patrol car."

"Well Tom, you better make that your only beer for the moment. Don't forget we've got to go down to Marion Bridge for Pappy Franks eighty-fifth birthday party tonight."

"Oh, nuts, I completely forgot. Is there any way you can go alone with Joey? You can claim that I have a headache or some other BS. The last thing I need right now is Pappy grouching all the time. I used to be one of his favorites until I joined the police, but now he looks at me like I'm some traitor to the working class. The last time I was down there, he greeted me by singing the *Internationale*, remember?"

Amanda, (who grew up in nearby New Waterford) was a descendant of Polish immigrant coal miners recruited from Silesia to work in the coal fields of New Waterford Coal and Iron, just chuckled.

"Even though Pappy was born in the 1930s, he certainly learned about the riots in New Waterford in 1925. Surely you remember William Davis, who was killed at the New Waterford Lake riot on June 11, 1925. Davis Day has come to symbolize both the miners' battle for fair wages and the continuing struggle to save Nova Scotia's coal industry. Even I got dirty looks when it was announced that you and I were going to marry. Memories are long about those strikes, and even today you won't find a coal miner going down into the pits on June 11."

"Yes, that's so. And I heard all those stories, just as you did, from the time I was in primary school until today. But it wasn't the Cape Breton Regional Police that murdered him; it was a private army of thugs and hoodlums that the owners dressed up in police uniforms. It had nothing to do with us."

"But you know Pappy. He's not into subtleties. But maybe we ought to get a move on if we want to get down to Marion Bridge before the party starts. Didn't old Pappy Franks used to take you fishing on the river there when you were a little boy?"

"Yes, he took me out along the Mira River. Some of the best days of my childhood were spent with him, and I'm sorry that he doesn't feel the same way about me anymore."

They bundled Joey into his car seat and set off for Marion Bridge, about a half hour away. And like all traditional Cape Breton house parties, it had started early and quickly flowed out into Jesse Franks spacious backyard.

When they arrived, Jesse's wife of nearly sixty years, Tom's Aunt Dorri, met them at the front door. She had the well-deserved reputation of being the only person who could contain Pappy Franks when he was on a tear, and yet everyone remarked that she didn't look much older than the day she married him, over a half-century before. She greeted them warmly and made a great fuss over little Joey.

Amanda had once made the mistake of asking her how many children, grandchildren, and great-grandchildren she and Pappy Franks had, and Dorri lost count at thirty-five. "There may be more," she said, "but I can't remember some of them who moved off to Fort McMurray to work in the tar sands of Alberta. I don't often see them, but little Joseph here – he's one of my favorites – aren't you Joseph Roy?"

Joey came and gave his great-aunt a big hug.

They all went out into the backyard and greeted Pappy. Surprisingly, he was quite cordial to both Tommy and Amanda. Holding a bottle of Moosehead Lager in one hand, he welcomed Tommy with "Just what the hell is this I'm hearing about those little girls being kidnapped up there in Glace Bay? Do you know anything about that Tom? Terrible-just Terrible."

"Yeah, I've been working on that since it happened. In fact, I believe I was the last police officer to see the school bus when it came through an accident site off Grand Lake Road. They're being held in the Miners Museum building, right between Caledonia and GB. And they have been there for a week, and nothing much is happening."

"Where do you think they're keeping the kiddies?" Pappy asked.

"We think they're in the old Imperial Coal's Shaft 19 which the museum uses as a tourist attraction, or at least the first couple hundred yards of it or so. But since they are apparently armed to the teeth and aren't threatening any harm to the kids just yet, the Mounties have us in a 'wait and see' mode. So we're in a siege around the museum."

"Yeah, that's about what you would expect the Mounties to say. Sometimes I think their horses are smarter than they are. But why don't you guys just go through one of the tunnels that intersect the old Imperial shaft? I know they're there, because back when I was about 18 or so, I worked for a bootleg coal outfit, and we used to sneak in there and 'rob the pillars' all around there. Hell, we made more money out of Imperial's coal than we did out of our own!"

"I'm not sure I know what you're talking about, Pappy. I've looked at every map and chart that we can find, and I didn't see any tunnel intersecting the Imperial shaft, either onshore or submerged. Are you sure that it was their tunnel that you intercepted?"

"Now, just sprag your wheels oncet Thomas; you've turned into a smart-arsed kid since you went on the Coppers."

Intercepting one of his passing grandchildren, Pappy pointed to three older fellows drinking beer on the other side of the yard. "MaryJane, go tell those three lads to come over here, would you?"

"Ah, Pappy my name is MaryAnne, but I'll be happy to go get them for you."

The three old coal miners wandered over and shook hands again with Pappy. "This young pup seems to think that I'm senile and don't know what the hell I'm talking about. I told him how we used to rob the pillars back in the day and that we got a lot of coal out of Imperial Pit 19 in particular.

The three old miners, Allie Shapiro, Hallie White and 'Big Chick' Freihofer nodded in agreement. "That money we made from robbing them pillars kept our families and us alive during those tough years. Remember what it used to sound like when we got the last pillars out from behind us, and the roof caved in? A darn good thing we knew where the escape holes were before the roof came down. It was right around, oh 1950 or so that we got chased out of their coal seam and had to go back to being good honest coal miners."

"That's when Big Chick and Hallie went off and trained as Dragermen. ('Dragerman' is a traditional name for a rescue worker in the mines. The name originates from Alexander Drager, a German scientist who invented the combination of a gas mask and an oxygen inhalator as a breathing apparatus for underground rescue workers.) They worked at the Springhill in 1958 and Westray in 1992 mine explosions and both saved a hell of a lot of lives."'

The two former Dragerman just nodded modestly.

"Ah Jesse, we only just did what any other good miner would do."

Not wishing to displease his great-uncle, Tommy Franks listened attentively as the four elderly miners reminisced about their escapades a half-century before.

"Ah, Jasus, it was some comical when we came up out of that rabbit hole, and ould Father Mauer of Saint Mary's spotted us, and damn near had a heart attack, thinking the Devil himself was after him. Covered in coal dust was we, and black as the mine itself, but we could've made better time, Jesse, if you hadn't been carrying a sack with a hundredweight of coal on your back!"

"That was a cold winter, that was, and we needed all the

coal we could get. Good quality coal too if I remember correctly; it burned hot and bright," Jesse laughed.

During a pause in the conversation, Tom snuck off and wandered around exchanging polite meaningless words with the various cousins and other relatives whose names he could never recall. After a decent interval, he found Amanda chatting with two elderly women, no doubt relatives or friends of Pappy Franks, and signaled her that it might the time to go. She extracted herself, using the excuse that it was near Joey's bedtime, and they soon bade their farewell to Aunt Dorri and returned home.

The next day, Tom's shift in the incident room/command center did not begin until 1 PM. He used the morning, though, to drive down to Caledonia and to explore the area around Saint Mary's. He walked around the field in a spiral pattern and, about 300 yards southwest of the rectory, he discovered a large rectangular concrete structure about 3 feet tall covered with weeds and faded graffiti. He made his way through the thick underbrush of sea oats and other vegetation, dodged rusty beer cans and other debris, and read the graffiti which included GBHS-'54 and 'Donal loves Jeanie' surrounded by a crudely drawn heart. The name 'Jeanie' however was crossed out, and the name 'Sharon' later spray painted underneath.

Using the GPS function of his cell phone, he identified the exact location as 46.19° N, 59.95° W and the azimuth from the rectory at approximately 175°. Returning to his car, he jotted down the precise location and returned home to shower and don his uniform before heading over to the command center. Tommy first approached his mentor, Sgt. McCann."I learned something last night from my Great Uncle which might be important. He claims that there is a disused bootleg tunnel running from Caledonia and crossing the old Imperial Shaft 19 while still on land. I think we ought to check that out."

Sgt. McCann agreed and approached Staff Sgt. Morrison with the message, who relayed it to inspector Pelletier who, although a Mountie was considered 'tame' by the working stiffs in the CBRP. Pelletier took the news to both senior officers present, and within fifteen minutes or so Tommy was standing in their august presence, explaining what he had learned.

"Here are the coordinates," he said, handing them a slip of paper. My Great Uncle claims that he and some of his 'marras' used to use that tunnel to sneak into Imperial 19 and steal coal. And, knowing my Great-Uncle and his three buddies, I do not doubt that what he said was true."

Commissioner Paisley spoke up. "This might be the breakthrough that we're looking for, Constable. Can you get any of these fellows to go down that shaft with you and see what you can find?"

"Well, I don't think so, sir, seeing as their average age appears to be about 105 – well not really – but they are certainly in their 80s, but I'm willing to go down there if we can get some experienced miners to go with me."

Commissioner Paisley responded. "I'll get Personel on the line immediately and have them search their files to see if we have any members of our department with experience in the mines. Seeing as the last mine closed about 1998, we may have one or two that worked in the mines before coming on the force. You've done a good job here, Constable Franks. This is probably the best news we've heard since the bus was hijacked a week ago yesterday."

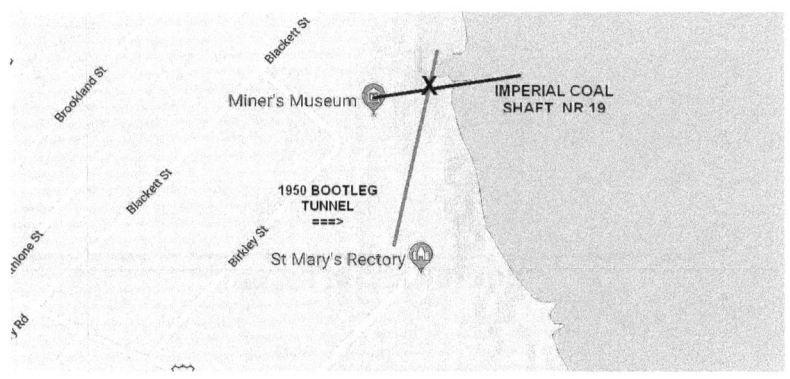

UNCLE JESSE'S EXCELLENT MEMORY

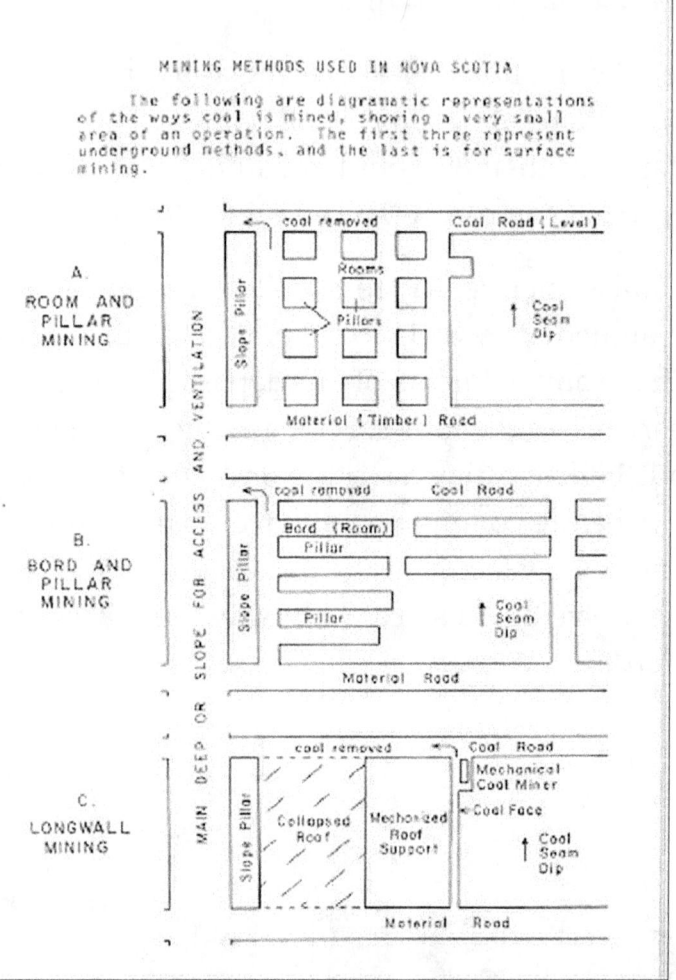

MINING METHODS USED IN NOVA SCOTIA

The following are diagramatic representations of the ways coal is mined, showing a very small area of an operation. The first three represent underground methods, and the last is for surface mining.

A.
ROOM AND PILLAR MINING

B.
BORD AND PILLAR MINING

C.
LONGWALL MINING

ROBBING THE PILLARS

CHAPTER SIXTEEN: WE RISE AGAIN IN THE FACES OF OUR CHILDREN

If Constable Tom Franks believed the atmosphere in the incident room to be the same old same-old,' he should have been with the twenty-three young dancers held unwillingly in the mine shaft. By Tuesday, the eighth day after the kidnapping, and with no end yet in sight, they had entertained themselves by singing the lyrics to many recent movies, including every song that they collectively recalled from Disney's *Moana, Mulan, The Little Mermaid, Frozen and the Lion King.* Even their four 'Guardian Angels': Fay, Kami, Sandy, and Mary were becoming concerned with the constant boredom of hostage life inside Imperial's Shaft 19.

But, the night is darkest just before the dawn, it is said. Starring off into space that morning, little Chloe Maguire, aged 12 from Chicago, happened to notice a sticker on the back of Kathy's boombox. She recognized the symbol and went over and looked at it more closely. She asked Kathy, "Did you know that your boombox is Bluetooth enabled?" Kathy, quite honestly had never noticed the sticker on the bottom of the boombox. "No, I haven't, but then I don't have a way to make a connection via Bluetooth. At least I don't think that I have."

Chloe went back to her sleeping bag and returned with her cell phone. "I know we have no reception down here in this mine shaft, but I have lots of Irish dancing music stored in memory, and it doesn't need to be connected to a network. Can we try to see if that will work through your boombox?" Kathy, desperate for anything to entertain her increasingly restless and despondent 'wards,' quickly agreed. It took them just a few minutes to sync the cell phone to the boombox and were rewarded by the strains of the 'Irish Washerwoman' resounding through the speakers of the Sony Boombox. And it was like magic; all the girls came running from the alcoves (and even the Porta Potties!) in response to the sounds of the familiar Irish tune.

When Chole and Kathy explained what they had done, several other girls retreated to their sleeping bags and retrieved their cell phones. All told, there were over a dozen cell phones, each one carrying twenty or more songs that the girls had used to practice before a Feis. It was just a matter of time until someone (in this case little Mia Flynn of Reno) came up with an obvious solution to the boredom of their captivity.

"Let's have a Feis of our own," she exclaimed. "We've got everything we need; we have jigs, reels, and hornpipes and we can stage our own Oireachtas right here in the mine! The hostages immediately perked up, and several asked if they could remove their Chadors so that they could dance in their costumes. Most of the girl's parents had been tasked with carrying their wigs, but nearly everyone had their small dancing bags with both their soft and hard shoes in them. Their most pressing problem at the moment was that they did not have a dance floor.

Kami and Fay, who had been attracted by the commotion, proposed a solution. Taking one of the 'Gators back to the portal, they soon returned with two large sheets of three-quarter inch plywood. Placed together, they made an acceptable substitute.

"But who are going to be the adjudicators?" Chloe asked plaintively. "We can't bring any judges down here, can we?"

"No, but we have two very experienced international dancers with us," Maura Lincoln replied. "How about Cora and Avid? They would make excellent judges!" Both international dancers quickly agreed.

Mary interjected. "Let's not do this right now because it's getting close to lunchtime. But after lunch, we'll sweep out an area behind the school bus. Kathy, you can put your boombox there on the back bumper, and it should be out of the way. But one thing we need to worry about is the battery life of your cell phones, so I suggest only one girl's cell phone be used each time you want to dance. That way, you'll keep the ability to dance at least once a day for the next week or so. Does that make sense to you?" All of the girls agreed, and it was a much happier lunchtime than had been seen for the last several days.

After lunch the hostages retired for a short siesta. But the excitement about the 'First Annual Underground Feis' was evident, and very quickly all of the young dancers were awake and arguing who would dance first.

"Well, why don't we treat this like a regular Feis back home?" asked Sophie Morgan of Denver. "We usually have the U-12 dancers first, followed with each older age group in turn. That way, the younger kids can watch how the older groups perform." All of the others agreed, and the U-12 dancers assembled off to the side of the homemade 'stage.'

"Hey, we need someone to be the musician for us. And what kind of tunes are we going to dance to?" asked Molly Lincoln.

"I'll be the musician," said Kathy. "I don't know anything about Irish dancing, but I do know how my boombox works." Everyone laughed and agreed.

The first two dancers took the stage. Kathy Khizrieva, with absolutely no idea which music was best for which occasion, randomly selected 'Fiddler Around the Fairytree,' a tune well-known and loved by the U-12 dancers. As the music began, the first pair began dancing, and the sound of their hard shoes on the plywood flooring resonated throughout the tunnel. It was almost as loud as if they had been on an official dancing platform.

Cora remarked to Kathy, "the U-12 dancers usually dance two numbers in each set. If you let me look throughout the playlist on the cell phone, I'll try to select appropriate music for each pair of dancers." "By all means!" chuckled Kathy. Cora, in addition to being one of the judges, now took responsibility as the musician.

Since there were ten dancers under the age of 12, and each dancer performed two dances, the girls danced for about a half hour. Then the U-14 dancers took over the platform and danced both jigs and reels with an occasional hornpipe thrown in for good measure. Finally the oldest group, the U-18's danced, but because there were considerably fewer of them and their stamina was usually greater, they danced together for about another half hour. Finally, came the moment of truth. It was time for the adjudicators to make their decisions!

Cora and Avid conferred. "This is going to be difficult, Avid," Cora said. "Whatever we do, we are going to hurt someone's feelings." "Let's declare a tie, and that way everyone in the 'World's First Underground Feis' will earn a medal. I have no idea where we could get a medal, but if we have some bottle tops lying around here, we could probably use those." Avid just laughed. "Sounds like a perfectly good Ozzie workaround," she said. Cora replied, "Okay Kiwi, you've got my back. But let me know if there is a revolution brewing and we'll come up with another plan, okay?"

But there was no revolution; in fact, the sense of hopelessness which had begun to overtake the hostages was relieved. And after dinner and their regular hygiene, everyone retired for the night, in a much happier frame of mind that when they had awakened.

Constable Tommy Franks arrived at the command center for his regular shift on Wednesday. About fifteen minutes after he came in, SSgt. Morrison stopped by his desk. "Well the Boss checked, and HR told him that we don't have anyone on the CBRP with mining experience.

"But there is some good news, though. The Cape Breton Regional Fire Service (CBRFS) has two full-time firefighters who had experience as miners before they joined the Fire Service. One of them is a Platoon Chief up in Sydney Mines; the other is a Fire Captain in North Sydney. We called, and both are willing to contribute if it helps free the hostages. Both guys will be down here around ten this morning and will be ready to go out in the field with you once you brief them on what you know. But these guys are not law enforcement. They can explore the bootleg tunnel, they will assist you in every way possible, but they can't participate in an assault. So go with them, explore the conditions in the tunnel, brief me, then I'll let the bosses know."

"The terrorists claim to have explosives primed and planted around the shaft, and we must keep those kids safe at all costs. When these guys arrive, we can figure which way we go from here."

Platoon Chief Charlie Koshue and Captain Terry Dennis of the CBRFS soon entered the command center and shook hands with Constable Franks. Both were in their early 60s and appeared to be remarkably physically fit.

"So, Constable, tell us what is it you learned about this possible tunnel crossing near imperial's Shaft 19?"

"My great-uncle told me a story Monday evening about bootlegging coal back around 1950 or so. I thought this was another "back in the day" story, but three of his friends were there and not only vouched for the story but added additional details. They'd been 'robbing pillars' from the Imperial mine and had used an intersecting shaft to get in; roughly a quarter-mile southwest of old

Saint Mary's Rectory. If what he says is true, the shaft intersects '19 on a diagonal, and I don't know if it's above, below or at the same level as Imperial's shaft. The other thing I don't know is where on land they intersect. It might be close to the pithead, or it could be 3 feet from the water's edge for all I know. But the bosses seem to think it's worth a look and we don't have anything else that sounds as promising."

"Well, let's go take a look," replied Chief Koshue. "We've brought along a lot of gear; incidentally, both of us had worked as Dragermen before the last mines in CB closed, and we've been called as far west as northern Ontario to help with mine rescues. If your great-uncle was robbing pillars, he was one lucky SOB; lots of miners have had tunnels collapse around them. But yeah, let's go; I've brought the CBRFS SUV from Sydney Mines where I'm working now. Terry here works at North Sydney, and his expertise is fire at sea. So whichever way this works out we've got it covered. Come on; you can ride with us."

It took about 20 minutes to drive from the CBU campus to the area where Tom had discovered the entrance to the ventilation shaft. They parked the fire vehicle on the road past the rectory and, carrying heavy-duty bolt cutters and a 24-foot extension ladder, walked to the ventilation shaft. They had no problem in finding the concrete structure.

"Yeah, that looks like your standard ventilation cover," Platoon Chief Koshue remarked. "let's see exactly what we're dealing with here. It's all probably caved in down at the tunnel level, but we won't know that until we get it open."

With one man on each side of the 8 foot bolt cutters, they easily removed the large padlocks that secured the structure. They soon had it clear and lying on the ground, and both shined their high power LED flashlights down the shaft.

"Hey I got a question for you guys," said Tommy. "If this is a ventilation shaft, where is the large fan that you would expect to see here?"

The two firefighters laughed. "Well if this was a bootleg shaft, the guys that dug it took anything that wasn't tied down when they finally left. Seventy years ago, the fan blades were usually solid brass, and you could get a pretty good price for 'em. The same with the electric motor; some guys would take those motors, rewind them and sell 'em on. It's like they say about pig farmers, they'd sell you everything except the squeal."

"You see that ladder going down the side, Constable? Don't trust that ladder at all, son. I bet those rungs wouldn't hold a kitten today. But it looks like it terminates about 20 feet or so down there, so that's where the horizontal shaft probably begins. By the way, we have helmets and extra breathing apparatus in the back of the SUV. The last thing you'd want to do is head down a coal hole like this without having any idea what you're going to find down there. Black damp, white damp, who knows? But let's not speculate, let's get down there and find out what we have."

" We can leave that cover off; it doesn't look like anyone's been here in the last 20 years and I don't expect anybody will fall in while we're down there." Terry inserted the extended ladder, while Chief Koshue looked around for rocks and tossed them down the shaft. They could hear them bouncing on the sides of the shaft as they fell, and also heard them land and Capt. Dennis estimated the bottom would support all three.

As he waited for two firefighters to assemble the ladder,and retreive their gear, Tom received a cellphone call from SSgt. Morrison, who informed him that Commissioner Paisley had spoken with the skipper of the CCGS GEORGE ANDREWS, which had located the seaward portion of Shaft 19. He offered to transmit active sonar pulses at low power every five minutes beginning at 12:30 PM. Tom repeated this to the firefighters while he donned their spare miner's hardhat and battery pack and high visibility LED light. He also slipped into his bright yellow CBRP rain suit and waited until Capt.

Dennis had descended the ladder and tested the atmosphere with his handheld Altair 4X Multi-Gas Detector.

Signaling all clear to Chief Koshue, the chief then directed Tom to descend the ladder first and that he would immediately follow.

All three reached the bottom of the shaft safely. To their left (southwest) there were signs of total collapse, but to their right (northeast) the tunnel extended well out of their visible range. All three crouched and began slowly moving forward. Aside from some fallen roof supports the way was clear, although the diameter of the tunnel required that they proceed in single file. With Capt. Dennis in the lead, Tom in the center and Chief Koshue bringing up the rear, they alternately crouched and crawled toward the expected intersection point. They stopped every five minutes, to both catch their breath in the damp and fetid atmosphere of the abandoned mine tunnel, but also to listen for the low powered ping expected from the CCGS GEORGE ANDREWS.

They progressed at a steady pace, and after about 25 minutes in the tunnel, Capt. Dennis signaled for silence. Very faintly, off to their right, they heard the high-frequency pings, indicating that they were very close to the predicted intersection point. They still did not know, however, if that tunnel was above or below the grade upon which they were progressing. The shaft was wider at that point, and so they crouched down together to discuss their next moves.

"We may be below the grade of the Imperial 19. But that's just a guess. The roof and sides here appear fairly safe; there's lots of iron ore here, which is not unusual in this part of the Nova Scotia coal fields," Chief Koshue told the others.

Just as he was speaking, Captain Dennis signaled for silence.

"Damn, I thought for a minute that I heard music. Yes, I do! It sounds like it's coming from our left side further on in the tunnel. Let's move up a little bit and listen again. I hope that's not angels I'm hearing here, Chief" quipped Capt. Terry. "I don't know the history of this bootleg tunnel, but if any miners lost their lives here, well..."

They crawled along for another hundred yards or so, and the music became louder. They could hear the rhythmic tapping of Irish dancers (Maura and Molly Lincoln and their now inseparable friend, Annie Riley) performing an energetic triple jig on the ad hoc dance floor. "Well unless someone has opened an underground dance hall, I think we found your target, Tommy," said Chief Koshue.

"I'll call this in when we see daylight again" replied Tommy. "Can you mark this spot, Chief?"

Chief Koshue reached into his backpack and produced a small can of incandescent orange paint. He sprayed the left side of the tunnel as far as his arm would reach in the cramped spaces.

"We had better be quiet going back out," whispered Capt. Terry. If we can hear them, they can hear us."

They moved as silently as they could given the rough conditions of the floor of the bootleg tunnel, and Tom was nearly exhausted when they arrived back at the ventilator shaft.

"Too many donuts from Tim Horton's, Constable?", the two firefighters, twice his age, laughed. Tom laughed too after he caught his breath.

"You've got to tell that great-uncle of yours that he has a hell of a memory, Tommy. I can see those guys breaking through into Imperial 19 in the dark of night and grabbing hundredweight sacks of coal and hauling them back down this long escape route to the outside world. Those were some great miners here in Nova Scotia in those days, Constable. Be proud of your uncle and his marras. It's a shame that it's all history," Captain Dennis sighed. "We will never see their likes again."

CHAPTER SEVENTEEN: GO, LABOR ON WHILE IT IS DAY

The 'three amigos' returned to the command center shortly after 3 PM, and Tom reported to SSgt. Morrison immediately. She greeted him warmly. "Well, I understand from your radio reports that you were successful in finding an access route to the tunnel. Excellent work indeed, Constable."

"Well I certainly couldn't have done it without the information we received, and not without the assistance of two experienced ex-miners. It's a tight squeeze, but I am certain that the hostages can make it through without assistance."

"Well there are a couple of other developments that have happened while you were away that may make things easier. The first is that one Mountie went back over to the Department of Natural Resources, and prevailed upon them to let him search through their archives again. I'm not sure that 'archives' is the right word; he describes it as being more like stacks and stacks of reports chucked into the basement of the building. But he did find something useful."

She handed Tom a folder labeled 'Abandoned Mine Openings" dated 1924. There were several large and detailed charts of the entire island inside, and Tom quickly located one detailing the Phelan coal seam, which extended between Glace Bay and Caledonia. It was clear that the "bootleg" mine shaft was not bootleg at all; the chart showed the tunnel was owned by the Jubilee Coal And Iron Company of Halifax, and that it did, in fact, intersect Imperial Coal's Tunnel 19.

"While this new data probably would have been helpful, still someone needed to get down there and make sure that the old shaft was still passable. But this does name the bootleg shaft that your Great Uncle described."

Tom studied the newly found map closely. "That may not be the most important discovery here, ma'am. We thought that the walls of the shaft we were crawling through were hard rock; either basalt or more likely, granite. But this map shows that the sides are part of the coal seam itself, and that makes sense. If my uncle Jesse was in there robbing pillars, it stands to reason that they were part of that coal seam, as narrow as it might have been. We marked the spot where we thought we were closest to Imperial's shaft 19, both by the strength of the pinging from the Coast Guard ship, but also by a most extraordinary set of circumstances. I did not want to mention this on the non-secure radio channel, but we were so close to the hostages that we could heard the young ladies dancing to Irish music inside the Imperial shaft. I doubt that we were any more than, say, twenty feet from that tunnel. And we heard them off to our left on our shore-ward side, meaning that we were not below the tidal line, which is, itself, very reassuring. If in fact the walls are the sides of the coal seam, it should make it that much easier for us to break through."

Staff Sgt. Morrison nodded. "Well, you've certainly done a good days work, Constable. Now I have some other news for you. The RCMP has summoned the combined Emergency Response Teams (ERTs) from New Brunswick, Prince Edward Island, and Nova Scotia. They are all on their way here now. They're also sending additional weaponry, both lethal and nonlethal, and within the last hour, I met with Inspector Pelletier, who believes it will be at least a fifty-person team, including ten or so female RCMP constables to assist with the hostages after the ERT breaches the tunnel. Things are definitely moving toward a climax, and we're holding the day shift here until 8 PM this evening. But I could make an exception for you; it appears that you've pretty much destroyed your uniform and if you would like to go home and change, you may. And do apologize to your wife for me, Constable."

"Thank you, ma'am, and I should be back here within the hour. Can we let the two firefighters know these new developments?" SSgt. Morrison thought for a moment. "I can't think of any reason why not; they knew what we're investigating and why. In fact, didn't you say that you could hear the hostages very close through tunnel wall? Go out and ask them if they would like to stay and assist if necessary, while I see Commissioner Paisley and ask him to contact the CBRFS and request their temporary assignment to us. Personally, I doubt this crisis will last another 24 hours, so I'm certain the Fire Service will concur."

Tom went back and spoke to the Chief and Fire Captain. Both readily agreed to stay on. "That's one more thing that you coppers don't understand about the Fire Service, Tom. We work 24 hours on and then 48 hours off duty. If we went back to our fire halls, we'd still be on duty until 8 o'clock tomorrow morning. We may as well stay here and be as helpful as we can."

After Constable Tommy Franks returned, freshly showered and in a clean uniform, he ran into his old partner and trainer, Sgt. Dan McCann. "I understand you're a minor league hero these days, Thomas. But one of these days you're going to have to learn how to conduct interviews with someone other than your relatives."

Tommy laughed. "Well, it's like how they teach insurance salesman. The first people you try to sell policies to are all your relatives. But for a guy his age his memory is excellent, and we found the ventilation shaft exactly where he said it would be. So I'm glad I could help out even a little. But I suppose I will go back to filing papers here and let the 'big boys' carry on."

"Don't be so sure of that Tom. This situation is about to climax in the next day or so, and everybody has a role to play. I understand that Commissioner Paisley got permission for your two buddies to stay here for the duration, and I also understand that he contacted the Salvation Army to set up camp beds and a portable kitchen to accommodate the ERT teams that will be here later this evening. Which, by the way, is exactly what you'll be doing when the Sally Ann trucks get here. I don't know if you know it, but the Commissioner is a longtime member of the Salvation Army, and his wife is an officer at the provincial level. We used to joke, before he became Commissioner, that he was outranked by his missus. But then again, most of our wives outranked us too."

Tommy laughed. "Yeah, my wife wasn't too happy to see the condition of my uniform when I got home. I wish they would increase the uniform allowance so that we can buy more than two sets at a time. If this set gets trashed, there'll be war in the cabin at the Franks household."

About an hour or so later, the Salvation Army trucks arrived and Tom and everyone else who was not occupied, pitched in assembling the camp beds, air mattresses and kitchen supplies for the expected RCMP personnel. Tom was working alongside Dan McCann. "Any idea who's going to be in charge of the actual hostage rescue, Dan?" Tommy asked.

"Yeah, I've heard some of the Mounties say it's going to be Chief Super. John Duffy. He's got the reputation of being a real fire-breather and is one of the few very senior Mounties who actually has a lot of relevant field experience. He's a mountain man from up around Thunder Bay, and his nickname is 'The Gladiator.' He was key to the success of that ERT rescue mission in Saskatchewan about 20 years ago. He was just a rookie – hopefully, smarter than you, Tom – but when those four Mounties were captured and killed by some crazy SOB in rural Saskatchewan, he held the fort until support arrived. The bosses thought so much of him that they sent him back to the Depot as an instructor, about the youngest Mountie ever to get that job in Regina, and certainly, the youngest ever to be awarded the Medal Of Bravery (MB) by the Queen. And every place else he's gone, he's gotten deep into operations and had done a fantastic job. Inspector Pelletier thinks he's on a fast-track to be their Commissioner in the not so distant future."

As Tom and Dan were chatting the incident room received word that a Canadian Forces CC-144 Challenger twin-engine jet, carrying five senior officers of the Emergency Response Command in Ottawa had landed at CFB Sydney River, and that a vehicle would deliver them to CBU within thirty minutes.

Tom, Dan and the others rushed the assembly of the cots and mobile kitchen and had them finished with a few minutes to spare. As scheduled, the team consisting of Chief Super. Duffy, and four inspectors arrive a few minutes later. Assistant Commissioner Rutherford and Inspector Pelletier, as the senior RCMP officers in the command center, greeted them as they entered.

Tom and Dan watched from the rear of the sleeping area. "Well it's not hard to tell who's in charge, is it Dan?" Tom whispered. "Yep, I never met him, but it's got to be the big guy with the short gray hair cut. Even though he's in civvies, he's a copper anywhere he goes," responded Dan. "The other four guys must be his horse holders."

"You don't want to mean they still ride horses, do you?" asked Tom, incredulously.

"No, that's just slang for the guys who carry his bags, make his tea and run his errands," responded Dan. "Let's get out of here; I never feel comfortable with big bosses around. Nothing good ever comes of that."

After exchanging greetings, Chief Super. Duffy introduced his four colleagues. Each one was responsible for a separate function of the ERT. "This is my deputy, Inspector Luc Morin; our chief negotiator, Inspector Alasdair Ross; our Tactician, Inspector Archibald Menzies and our Armorer, Inspector Grant Jones. I spoke to the senior officers of each of the three division teams while we were in the air; the 'H' division team from Halifax is less an hour away, the 'J'division team from Moncton is about thirty minutes behind them, and the 'L' team from Prince Edward Island will be here at about 11:30 PM. They got a slow start because of heavy winds on the Confederation Bridge."

"Under the circumstances, there is no way that I would suggest running this operation tonight. It's best run during the hours of darkness, and we would only have about five hours to get everything in place before sunrise. We'll use tomorrow for planning and run-throughs, and then make entry at about 0100 the following morning. I understand that you have some former miners lined up to assist us?"

Commissioner Paisley, who had joined the conversation spoke up. "Yes that we do, CS Duffy. We have two experienced miners; both are former Dragermen with plenty of experience in mine rescue, who now work for the Cape Breton Regional Fire Service and are loaned to us for the duration. They were down in the 'rescue' tunnel with one of my constables earlier today, and in fact, could hear the voices of several of the hostages clearly from inside that disused mine tunnel."

CS Duffy nodded and remarked, "Let me give you an idea of the plan that Luc and I dreamed up flying across from Ottawa. I assume that any digging into the tunnel where the hostages are held is going to generate a fair amount of noise. So I contacted CFB Shearwater and asked to borrow several CH-147F Chinook helicopters for a couple of hours tomorrow afternoon. The weather forecast shows that it is going to be a rainy day, but with very little wind, and in the rain the Chinooks make a lot of noise, particularly if the pilot sets the double rotors a little out of sync. We'll have 'em overhead about noon tomorrow, and even flying well outside the danger zone the noise from the choppers should mask whatever noise the miners make, provided they do it as quietly as humanly possible."

Paisley nodded.

"Well, we did get some handy information earlier today. We found charts of both tunnels showing the intersection points. The rescue tunnel crosses Imperial Coal's Shaft 19 about 6 feet below on a diagonal angle of about 45°. The better news is that both coal companies used the room-pillar method of supporting the overburden, and we believe that the only thing separating the tunnels is a single pillar of coal. Even using a pick and shovel, two experienced miners should be able to break through within an hour, and we estimate that the space occupied by the hostages is between 30 and 40 feet away from where the opening will be made. If we make sure that there is no light leakage through the opening, and we can do that with heavy black canvas which we will carry into the shaft, we shouldn't be detected."

"I've got to commend you and your department, Commissioner. I did learn that our Anti-Terrorism Squad attempted to enter the compound last Friday evening, but were dissuaded by being targeted by the hostage holders. That's a debacle that I will discuss with their team leader and with his chain of command when I get back to Ottawa."

Just then, a vehicle carrying the Nova Scotia divisional ERT team pulled up to the front door, and about 20 members of the province-wide group entered the command center. Their commander came and spoke with the group of senior officers.

Duffy responded. "Okay, SSgt, here's what I want you to do. Get your men fed if necessary and then bedded down. Reveille will be at 0630, and we'll hold our first briefing at 0800."

"Commissioner Paisley, can you have one or two of your men stand by here in the command center to pass that same message to the New Brunswick and P.E.I teams when they arrive? Reveille at 0630, briefing 0800. We'll need the miners sometime shortly before noon."

CHAPTER EIGHTEEN: AND HOME I'LL BE

Promptly at 0800 the next morning, CS Duffy greeted the ERT members, grouped by division in the bleachers. Joining them were several members of the CBRP who would perform vital support functions during the takedown of the terrorists.

"I don't want to be redundant with the things I discussed before, but for those of you who arrived later, be aware that we have an airborne distraction planned, with a squadron of CH-147F helicopters deployed as noisemakers to mask the breaching of the tunnel. They will arrive on station shortly after noon. So time is limited, and I'll address that which needs to be done between now and then."

First, to our colleagues in the CBRP; I understand from Commissioner Paisley that you have asked Rogers Communications of NS to park several vehicles near the portal of the rescue tunnel. I also understand that they will provide a small work tent to cover the portal and that they have been instructed to inform any bystanders that they are engaged in routine cable work. CBRP will also provide constables as a liaison at Glace Bay General Hospital to protect the hostages from the expected media onslaught. The hospital and the local ambulance services are on alert so that they might efficiently transfer the hostages to the hospital. Inspector Ross of my team has also arranged for field telephones to be installed from the entrance portal of the rescue tunnel to the breach point where we enter the hostage's area. That tunnel wireline will be manned at the portal by a CBRP team who will also be in constant encrypted communications with the command center. Now let me turn the meeting over to my deputy, Inspector Luc Morin."

Inspector Luc Morin stepped to the podium. "I have the team assignment for this evening's operation," he said, passing a stack of papers to the two constables seated closest to him. "I realize that you are all experienced operators, and we have made sure that each team contains only individuals from a single division with one exception. That exception is Team Number Four, the hostage care and recovery team. This team is composed of experienced female constables representing all three of the divisions on this assignment. My only comments, then are directed at them."

"You have perhaps the most important role of everyone here. All of us are experienced ERT operators; this may well be the only time that you're called to assist us on the front lines. But your job is tremendously important. These children range in age from 11 to 18, and they are no doubt traumatized by the events of the last ten days. It's up to you that, regarding of whatever else is going on, you maintain your calm in the face of chaos. These kids are going to be very frightened when you wake them shortly after midnight. I suggest that each of you fasten a small transparency of the Maple Leaf to your headgear."

Commissioner plays Paisley interrupted. "I will have my men generate a high-resolution photograph and printed it on adhesive paper to facilitate that task. We should have them for you well before lunch today."

"That will work quite well, Commissioner, and thank you for your assistance. You may ask 'Why do we not just wear the Red Cross or another insignia such as the St. John's Ambulance on a brassard?' And the answer to that is simple. They never carry firearms; you will be armed, carrying the service weapon that your division assigned to you at all times that you are involved in this operation. We want to remind these young ladies that we represent Canada and freedom from terror to the greatest extent possible. But I will not place you or any constables in any unnecessary danger."

"As for the rest of the teams, the tasks are self-explanatory. Team 3A will deploy at noon today to provide support and security for the former miners who will make the breakthrough between the rescue tunnel and Imperial Coal's Shaft 19. No doubt, they will ask you to assist them by carrying some of their equipment forward, and I expect that you will comply cheerfully and without question. At the completion of this first task, you'll return here and redeploy later as 'first over the top'. That's all that I have for you at the moment. Inspector Grant Jones will now discuss the armaments that we will use in taking down the terrorists. Inspector Jones?"

Inspector Jones, the armorer at ERT headquarters in Ottawa, and responsible for all firearms deployed by Emergency Response Teams nationwide stepped forward.

"Gentleman, If you would, please consult the single sheet of paper which just was passed to you. You'll see that there are seven teams formed for this assignment, and to keep matters simple, we're assigning the same armament for each separate position in the "stack" for most teams. The exceptions are the perimeter protection and hostage extraction teams."

"In general, each team will be headed by a senior sergeant, and he will assume the position of leader of his stack. The number one position, like every position, will carry the sidearm issued to him by his division. The operator in position number one will also carry the MP5/10 submachine gun, while the operators in positions two will deploy with the Colt M4 carbine and positions three and four will carry the Remington 87012 gauge shotgun. The operator in position five is designated as the non-lethal officer and will be equipped with dispensers of Pepper Spray [OC] and Tear Gas (Cs) and will also be equipped with a high voltage Taser."

"The only exception to this will be team number one whose role is to prevent and interdict anyone attempting to leave the compound once we have reached the tunnel wall. All members of the perimeter team will be equipped with the Remington 700 sniper rifle and will replace their normal sidearm with the Bren10 10mm Auto pistol. All of these armaments and sufficient ammunition are being delivered now by RCAF aircraft to CFB Sydney River and will arrive here under strong military escort no later than 1400 today. The only other comments I have for you are these: we have been briefed by the intelligence community that at least one, and possibly several of the Chechen terrorists are experienced fighters in Bosnia and Herzegovina, as well as their revolt in Chechnya. These are experienced warfighters, and you should not expect an easy time of it today."

"In a situation such as this, they can face only one of four outcomes: surrender, our use of less-lethal force, our use of deadly force, or escape. There is only one acceptable outcome, and that is ideally the peaceful surrender of the terrorists and the safe extraction of the hostages whom they hold. Good luck to you all, and finally, a few words from our Tactician, Inspector Archie Menzies before we disperse."

"Thank you, Inspector Jones. I see that CS Duffy is signaling me to hurry up, and I will move on as quickly as I can. But there is one piece of information which we have learned from the intelligence communities both here in Canada and in the States that might moderate your concerns about the operation we're about to undertake. After much investigation by both agencies working together, they have determined with a high degree of certainty that no one has purchased or stolen gelignite in the last ninety days. That's the stability limit of that particularly volatile explosive. While the Chechens have stated that they have planted explosives throughout the mines, it would be difficult to do so using gelignite that is old and unstable. And if their claims about the gelignite are false, we can consider with a high degree of certainty that their claims about C-4 are also invalid. But just to be sure, team 3B will be tasked with the close inspection of the interior of the mineshaft after we breach the dividing wall. Team 3B will also be issued brass tools to assist in the safe dismantling of any explosives or incendiary devices which may have been deployed by the terrorists. But our best estimation now is that this is just hyperbole and a bluff on the part of the hostage takers. CS Duffy?"

CS Duffy returned to the podium. "It is now well after 0930, and the first element of this assault will take place concurrent with the arrival of the helicopters in about 2

1/2 hours time. At this point, I turn each of the teams over to their senior NCO for discussion and rehearsal of their separate roles."

After loading two CBRP SUVs with the necessary tools and equipment to connect the rescue tunnel to Imperial Shaft 19, Tom and Sgt. McCann each drove one vehicle to the agreed upon "muster point" about 100 yards east of the rescue tunnel portal. Chief Koshue and Captain Dennis arrived a few minutes later and remained in their vehicle until the rain let up. As Sgt. McCann drove up in the second vehicle they were also met by three cable service vehicles of Rogers Communications. Tom asked that they erect the 12x12 Ft. work tent over the cover of the ventilation shaft, and a few minutes later, everyone had a haven from the intermittent rain.

"I think we have everything you fellas asked for," Tom reported to Chief Koshue. "We also have the additional folding ladder that you say you needed. I'm not quite sure where that plays in this dig, however."

"Captain Dennis replied. "Suppose you wanted to knock a hole between two rooms of your house. With a good sledgehammer, it probably would take you fewer than fifteen minutes. But now suppose you want to knock a hole between your living room on the first floor and your bedroom on the second. The first thing you would have to do is make sure that you are aligned correctly, and that's going to be our first task when we're attempting to breach Imperial Shaft 19. That's where the fiber optic viewing scope as well as the wired microphone we asked for come into play. We'll drill a tiny hole into the ceiling of the rescue tunnel, and then check to see how close we're to the center of shaft 19. If not, we'll move left or right or back and forth until we get where we want to be. Then, using the 'Little Monster' folding ladder, Charlie and I will begin to widen the hole to the point where a man can get through. We'll use the folding ladder, first as a platform from which to work, and then extend it between tunnels so that the rescue team can get up and the hostages and constables can get back down."

Just then they faintly heard the sound of the four helicopters from CFB Shearwater arriving on the scene. By the time they took station, flying a racetrack pattern about two miles away from the museum, they certainly were loud enough to make conversation difficult, so with the assistance of Team 3A, the group manhandled the concrete cover, and inserted the fire department ladder into the shaft. Distributing the various tools and equipment to the team 3A members, one by one they descended into the ventilation shaft. The last team member carried a spool of telephone wire, one end of which was connected to the first field phone which Sgt. McCann had brought along from the command post. Because of the varying clearance of different sections of the rescue tunnel, they were sometimes able to walk upright; they crouched and 'duck walked' for part of the journey, and finally crawled the remainder of the way until they spotted the incandescent orange painted mark they had made on their previous exploration. They connected the wire to the second field telephone and established communications with the portal crew. The total journey took about fifteen minutes; about half as long as their first trip through the 'bootleg' shaft.

The two Dragermen quickly assembled the portable platform, and Captain Dennis took the first turn using the three-foot coal auger powered by a 24-volt high-capacity battery. "I never could figure why they called this 'soft coal,'" thought the former miner to himself. "Anybody who tries to cut through this will soon realize that it's anything but soft." He continued the drilling, replacing the shaft every few minutes with a longer extension. At long last, he felt the tip of the bit breaking through. He withdrew the drill and asked chief Koshue to disassemble it.

"Pass me up the fiber-optic scope, Chief, and let me see what we have up here." Chief Koshue soon handed it to him on the platform, and he inserted it through the four-inch diameter hole which he had just drilled.

"Well I'll be damned," Capt. Dennis whispered to his partner. You'll never guess what I just found!" He changed positions with the platoon chief who checked the monitor and laughed aloud. "How in the world did they get that school bus down this far in the shaft? It looks like there's about a foot of clearance on either side, which is going to make it difficult for the rescue parties to get through. But there's nothing we can do about that; if we tried to come up behind the school bus, we run the risk of hitting the gas tank, which would be about the worst result I can imagine. We'll have to trust the rescue team to know what they're doing."

Capt. Dennis and the chief traded places yet again.

"Do two things for me, if you will," he said. "Ask the guys at the portal to contact the choppers; this is about the time we need them to make as much noise as they can. And pass me up that short handle pick and get everyone out of the way. I'm going to start enlarging this hole to man size. Everyone stay clear below; there's going to be a lot of coal and rock coming down as soon as I start whacking at this overburden. Stay back at least 20 feet and extinguish any lights. If the Chechens come exploring to find out what's the noise, we don't want them seeing the light shining from below."

It took far less time than they had estimated to make the hole wide enough an adult to pass from tunnel to tunnel. As the rubble began to fall, Chief Koshue directed the members of Team 3A to help clear the debris and to make the path as smooth as possible, not only for their retreat but also for the advance of the rescue parties later that evening. About ninety minutes after entering the rescue tunnel, they had the black tarpaulin in place blocking the light from the rescue shaft and began the long slog back to the rescue portal.

After the team returned safely back to the surface, Sgt. McCann, using the encrypted radio system, notified the command post that they could dismiss the four helicopters to return to Shearwater. As the last helicopter, containing the squadron commander passed overhead, he dipped the nose of the chopper to the officers in silent homages to dangerous rescue attempts now just a few hours away. Then, packing the gear and the tools, everyone returned to the command center, leaving two other CBRP constables to guard the scene until later that evening.

Once back at the command center, Ssgt. Henry MacFain briefed the senior officers on what they had discovered. As the leader of Team 3B, he had an excellent understanding of what had been done and what would need to be done by the rescue party when they arrived in

Shaft 19 later that evening.

"I see two major difficulties which the teams are going to face. The first is that the rescue shaft, although ostensibly safe, is difficult to traverse even without carrying assault weapons, ammunition, and personal protection equipment. We can only walk upright about one-third of the distance between the portal and the breached wall separating the tunnels. The second issue is the school bus which is blocking the occupied tunnel. The two firefighters estimate that there is a foot or less of clearance between the sides of the school bus and the walls of the tunnel. That's the bad news. The good news is that the school bus acts as a natural shield protecting the operators behind it."

"Personally, I think we should be able to make our way around the school bus without too much difficulty, but I have another suggestion. Just like every school bus in Canada, this one has an emergency door at the rear. Were we to open the front door, walk back through the school bus and out the back door we would avoid trying to squeeze heavily armed operators around the bus. As an adjunct to that suggestion, I recommend that we change the order of entry slightly. We have the assault teams going in first and the hostage protection teams going in later. I'd suggest we send a "slimmed down" assault team accompanying the hostage rescue team first. Since we've learned from the intelligence gathered from the young girl taken to the hospital that there was perhaps a ten minute ride from the area where the girls are held up to the portal, I would suspect that the number of "minders" for the hostages is limited and if we can hold the element of surprise for as long as we can, we can evacuate the hostages the way we came in."

CS Duffy and his four staff inspectors, as well as the senior members of the CBRP discussed this news at length. On the one hand, most believed in the axiom 'Plan The Work – Work The Plan,' but also realized that no plan is ever perfect and as soon as it is executed it's subject to change on the fly. After weighing the pros and cons, Duffy made his final decision. "Let's do it MacFain's way."

The change in plans was communicated to all team leaders, and after a light supper and last-minute briefing, all teams traveled in several blacked out vehicles to the rescue tunnel portal. The CBRP officers standing guard at the entrance assisted them down the ladder at 0030 local time, and they were assembled in the rescue tunnel at about 0050. All that was necessary now was the 'GO' signal transmitted via the field telephones from the portal to the breach point.

After final discussion, not only with the teams on the ground but with the ERT Command Center in Ottawa speaking with the authority of the Prime Minister himself, Duffy gave the GO signal at two minutes before 1 AM Atlantic Daylight Time. The signal was relayed, and the first operators, who had been re-purposed as protection for the hostage evacuation team, entered Shaft 19 only a minute or so behind schedule. They quickly forced the door on the school bus, ran to the back of the bus and opened the emergency exit, and then assisted the remainder of the first element to move forward.

About fifty feet into the tunnel, they spotted a visible guard nodding in a straight chair outside of the sleeping alcove holding the hostages. She was quickly overcome, handcuffed with plastic handcuffs and quietly hustled back through the school bus and down the shaft to the rescue tunnel where she was escorted to the entrance.

Team 4, the hostage rescue unit, headed by SSgt. Bradi Gagne and SSgt. Rita Ross slipped into the sleeping chamber and gently awakened the hostages.

"Don't be afraid girls, we're all Canadian police officers, and we've come to rescue you. Please, for your safety stay silent and follow our directions and we will very soon have you back to your families." Although some of the younger girls were obviously frightened, and one or two were crying softly to themselves, they were real troopers, and every one did what they needed to end their involuntary captivity. By 0120, all of the hostages were through the school bus, and by 0130 all were in the rescue tunnel in route to freedom.

Inspector Luc Morin, who was acting as on-site commander, and who was in constant contact with CS Duffy, confirmed that he had personally counted twenty-three young female hostages as they passed him in the rescue tunnel. He also notified Duffy that the girls appeared all to be identically dressed in black Chadors, and warned the ERT teams still in the pit that they were not in any way to be confused with the terrorists.

When Inspector Morin was sure that every hostage was safe, he directed the modified operation to continue and teams Two, 3B and Five proceeded quickly up the ladder, through the bus and moved toward the terrorist concentration at the head of the tunnel.

When they reached the area where the terrorists had been reported, there was no gunfire nor resistance from the surprised and sleeping terrorists, who quickly surrendered.

The leader of team Team 3B, SSgt. Vincent Murphy forcefully interrogated the Chechens about the explosives which they had claimed to have mined the tunnel. Ali Nuradilov spoke for his comrades. "I am the commander of this detachment of the Chechen Brotherhood, tasked with bringing the plight of our people to the attention of the entire world. This we have done, and I am proud of our actions and proud of my companions. But on my honor as a military officer, I promise you that there are no explosives in this tunnel. It was necessary for us to use that deception to bring the plight of our suffering women and children to the attention of the "free world." Again on my honor as an officer, I tell you that we would never harm your children, even though Russia continues to harm and kill our own."

The teams already in the tunnel made sure that there were, indeed, no explosives to injure them, and then on directions from CS Duffy, herded the handcuffed and hooded terrorists, both male and female through the front door of the museum to face the wrath and justice of the Canadian people.

CHAPTER NINTEEN: FAREWELL TO NOVA SCOTIA

The wrath of the Canadian people and the western world had indeed been aroused. Ten members of the Chechen brotherhood, six men and four women, who had been captured at the Miners Museum/Imperial Shaft 19, were carefully searched by RCMP Constables. They were then transported in the blacked out vehicles to their new temporary lodging, the Central Nova Scotia Correctional Facility at Burnside.

The major television networks had been caught off guard; the first indication that a rescue had been achieved was spotted by a technician monitoring their pooled long-range camera directed toward the Museum. Because of the massive cordon of armed police surrounding the crime scene, no field reporters had been able to approach within a mile of the building. As morning broke, RCMP Deputy Commissioner Arthur Rutherford and CBRP Commissioner Samuel Paisley, backed by Chief Superintendent Duffy and the members of his team, briefed the reporters at a hastily arranged press briefing in the parking lot of the museum.

"I am pleased to inform you that shortly after 0100 ADT this morning, a combined Emergency Response Team of RCMP personnel from all Maritime Provinces, with the assistance of both the CBRP and the CBRFS, and based upon information provided by the public, breached the

Imperial Coal Company Shaft 19 where twenty-three young hostages were being held."

"All hostages are being treated at Glace Bay General Hospital and are well and resting comfortably. Their parents are with them, and we expect that they will be discharged to them as soon as our inquiries are completed. There were no casualties among the terrorists who were holding them. The hostages were removed silently through a rescue tunnel identifies by private citizens and explored by the Cape Breton Police and Fire Services. Ten terrorists, six male, and four female were in the mine shaft at the time we breached Shaft 19, and all have been transported to the Central Nova Scotia Correctional Facility at Burnside. While I cannot tell you what charges will be leveled against them, you can rest assured that at the very least they will be charged with felony kidnapping and transporting these young ladies against their will."

"We will have more information for you after we complete a formal review of the this morning's operation, but again I commend and thank all members of the ERTs from the three provinces, and commend the assistance provided by the Cape Breton Regional Police Service. We will hold another briefing at 6:00 PM.We expect to be able to answer your questions then."

In the interval, the blacked out vehicles had first stopped at the RCMP headquarters on Victoria Street, and the male and female suspects were segregated in two additional prison-transport vans. Upon arrival at Burnside Correctional Facility, they remained segregated, and after in-processing, they were individually interrogated by teams of RCMP investigators, under the active supervision of Joshua Hamlin, the Chief Crown Attorney in the Office of Public Prosecution for Nova Scotia. All suspects freely admitted their affiliation with the Chechen Brotherhood, and all confessed to their participation in the hijacking of the school bus and holding its passengers without their consent.

Within 36 hours, a formal 'Information' had been prepared by the team of interrogators, and a preliminary hearing was held by Justice of the Peace Brendon Ryan, and a true bill of indictment was returned. After review by the Chief Crown Attorney, it was determined that only one of the suspects, Rudolf (Rudy) Kadyrov had actually performed the illegal act of kidnapping, thus violating Article 279, Section 1 of the Revised Statues by 'being a person who commits an offense by kidnapping a person or persons against their will'.

All six men had, however, 'caused the person or persons to be confined or imprisoned against the person's will by use of a restricted firearm or prohibited firearm in the commission of the offense,' in violation of Article 279, Section 2 of the Revised Statutes of Canada. Since Canadian law strongly favors prosecution of all criminal acts at a provincial level whenever possible, the Chief Crown Attorney assigned the case to the Superior Court of Nova Scotia, and in due course, the prosecution was assigned to The Honourable Anne K. Dellinger QC, at The Law Courts on Upper Water Street in Halifax.

Since The Canadian Legal Aid Program provides for the delivery of Public Security and Anti-terrorism (PSAT) legal aid services to economically disadvantaged persons subject to terrorism prosecutions, legal representation of all defendant 's was assigned to the law firm of Mullins, Stone and Sacramento and the trial date was scheduled for November 5.

Pretrial negotiations began immediately after the assignment of courts and counsel. The public defender's office submitted a plea bargain agreement by which the six male defendants would plead guilty and present no defense. The major points of the agreement included:

That the trials of the four female defendants be severed from that of the male defendants:

That every defendant, male or female, Canadian citizen or Landed Immigrant, be guaranteed that they would not be extradited nor deported to any country either during or after incarceration,

That Ilyas Tchermoeff, although eighteen years of age at the time of the offense be treated as a juvenile, and any incarceration be served in an appropriate juvenile or young offenders facility,

And finally, that Ali Nuradilov, as 'commander' of the Brotherhood be permitted to make a "speech from the dock," not subject to cross-examination, regarding the political situation surrounding Chechnya and their neighboring countries.

The Honorable Justice Anne K. Dellinger took the plea bargain under advisement, and after consultation with the Law Society of Canada accepted the agreement. The agreement was signed by Jack Stone of Mullins, Stone and Sacramento, the public defenders and Crown Attorney Joshua Hamlin shortly before the trial date in early November. On the day of the trial, the sealed agreement was made public and Justice Dellinger pronounced sentencing on the six male defendants:

Ali Nuradilov was sentenced to twenty years to be served at the Millhaven Institution at Bath ON.

Adlan Sheripov, Khasan Dudaev, Movsar Basayev, and Ali Nuradilov were sentenced to sixteen years at Millhaven.

Ilyas Tchermoeff was sentenced to three years at the Springdale Youth Centre in Brampton ON.

=/=

Severing the male and female cases provided the women's defense team with an opportunity to negotiate a better plea deal. The trial date of December 3 had already been set and Deputy Crown Attorney Shamilla Kaur and the trial judge, The Honourable Justice Julia St. Germain had already been named. Toni Sacramento, QC of Mullins, Stone, and Sacramento was the lead barrister for the defense. The prosecution and defense teams soon met.

"We have two major issues to discuss with you today," Toni Sacramento opened. "The first is that the charges laid against these four defendants are absurd. There's no evidence that these four young women had any part in planning or the kidnapping of these hostages. We submit that the charges of 'Acting As Accessories After The Fact of a Felony' as stated in Article 23, Section 1 of the Criminal Code Of Canada are more appropriate. We will stipulate to a prima facie case that they knew a crime had been committed and and intended to aid the principal offenders. If you modify the charges, we will propose a plea bargain allowing these defendants to plead guilty." The Chief Crown Attorney agreed.

Lastly, we beg leave to present videotaped depositions from a very few of the hostages. These will run no more than ten minutes each, and we can complete this trial within a single day." Again the crown prosecutor's office accepted the conditions. Sidebar, Ms. Kaur remarked, "Toni, why no extradition or deportation in the agreement? We already agreed to that with the men."

Toni Sacramento laughed. "Believe it or not, all are native-born Canadians; some even second or third generation. One is a registered nurse, another a schoolteacher, the third a university student, and one is the daughter of a former mayor in Ontario."

The trial began on December 3. The prosecution provided several witnesses who described in detail the conditions inside Imperial Shaft in 19 at the time of rescue. The RCMP witnesses conceded that although conditions were primitive, the hostage-takers had made every allowance for the comfort and safety of the young women.

When the prosecution rested, Ms. Sacramento began the videotaped depositions. Cindy Moore, age 12, of South Bend, related how Maret (Mary) Vakhaeva, RN had purchased a rescue inhaler for her asthma when her own had run out. Ellie Nolan, age 12, of Hartford explained that first day, everyone was asked if she had any medical issues. When she reported that she had type I diabetes, Nurse Vakhaeva arranged transportation to Glace Bay

General, although she knew this would result in the premature disclosure of their location. And, in an emotional ten minute video tape, the Lincoln family described in detail how Maura and Molly had been affected. "At first, they had trouble sleeping, and were afraid to ride the bus to school. But soon things got back to normal and soon they were praying for the Chechens, especially for the four women who helped them. Now, they are looking forward to seeing their twenty-two 'best friends' at various Feiseanna. And just the other day asked if we could help them organize a get-together! All kids this age are resilient; our two, having each other for support when held in the mine,seems more so than others."

After final arguments were heard, Justice Julia St. Germain retired to her chambers but returned with her verdict at 3:00 PM. She began, "It is clear from the evidence before me that each of you acted compassionately toward the young women who were placed in your charge. Nevertheless, your compassion was the 'fruit of a poisoned tree' in that it occurred during the ongoing commission of a felony. Neither compassion or your understandable zeal to relieve the sufferings of the Chechen people can provide complete mitigation of the crime of aiding and abetting this act of terrorism. Did you ever at any time during this ten day period consider the impact, not only on these young women but their families and friends? Did you consider the millions of Canadians and others who followed, and I might say prayed, for a speedy end to their captivity? Canadia is nation of laws. You yourselves are Canadian citizens by the right of birth. While I understand the factors which cause you to act as you did, that does not relieve you of the responsibility of acting in accordance wth the law."

"Fatima Dudaeva, Kamila Khizrieva,Maret Vakhaeva and Khadimat Yandarbiyeva: It is my sentence that each of you be committed to the Nova Institution for Women in Truro, for a period of one the year and one day each. I will grant you credit for the days that you have been incarcerated at Central Nova Scotia Correctional Facility at Burnside and hope that during your stay at Truro you reflect not only on the events that occurred in August, but also the horrendous outcomes which might well have resulted." And with that, she rose from the bench, bowed to counsel and left the courtroom.

JUSTICE JULIA ST GERMAIN Q.C

GLOSSARY

Abandoned Mines: The eastern portion of Cape Breton is undermined with mine tunnels, many of which appear on no maps nor charts.

Adjudicator: Tradition title for a Feis or Oiereachtas judge.

Alcove: Small side space in mines using the room and pillar configuration.

Alligator: (Gators) The John Deere Gator Turf Utility Vehicles.

Barging: Interfering with another dancer on stage.

Bodhran: Goatskin Drum used in Celtic music.

Bootleg Mine: Usually an abandon tunnel where unauthorized mining takes place.

Caledonia: Small Cape Breton community between Glace Bay and Donkin.

Callback: Those dancers who perform well receive a 'callback' for further prize competition at a Feis or Oireachtas.

Camogie: Women's stick and ball game, similar to hurling.

Cape Breton: A large island, northeast of the main portion of Nova Scotia.

CBRFS: Cape Breton Regional Fire Service.

CBRP: Cape Breton Regional Police [Service].

CBU: Cape Breton University.

CCG: Canadian Coast Guard.

CFB: Canadian Forces Base.

Chador: A full-body-length semicircle of fabric that is open down the front.

Chechnya: Federal republic of Russia located in the North Caucasus, situated in the southernmost part of Eastern Europe, and within sixty miles of the Caspian Sea.

William Davis: Coal miner killed in June,1925 during a mining strike near the town of New Waterford on Cape Breton. The date of his death is a legal holiday in Cape Breton.

Dragerman: Common name for a rescue worker in mines. The name originates from Alexander Dräger, a German scientist who invented the combination of a gas mask and an oxygen inhalator as a breathing apparatus for underground rescue workers.

Feis: (pl. Feiseanna) [Pronounced Fesh'] An Irish folk festival or convention patterned on the ancient feis and featuring games and competitions and usually traditional Irish music and dancing.

FIR: Irish word for 'MEN' Helpful to know when seeking a restroom!

Fire Hall: Canadian jargon for what, in the U.S., is a Firehouse.

Hornpipe, Jig, Reel: Most common forms of Irish step dancing seen in Feisanna or Oireachtais competitions.

Hurling: A stick and ball game, the national game of Ireland.

Imperial Coal Company: A fictional coal company set in eastern Cape Breton.

Ingushetia: A republic, located in the North Caucasus region, which annexed Chechnya in 1991.

Louisbourg: Founded by the French in 1713, this reconstruction of the original French town and fortifications is the largest of its kind in North America.

Maritimes: is a region of Eastern Canada consisting of three provinces: New Brunswick, Nova Scotia, and Prince Edward Island (PEI).

Marra: A work colleague; an equal. Term originated in County Durham in NE England, and was transplanted to Cape Breton.

Maura and Molly: Daughters of Erin and Pat Lincoln, and who are our fictional "stars". Their last names have been changed to protect the innocent!

Fort Mcmurray: Located in northeast Alberta, in the middle of the Athabasca oil sands, a significant destination for migrant workers from the Maritimes.

Mi'kmaq: First Nations people indigenous to the Maritimes.

Miners Museum: Located on one of the most picturesque coasts of Cape Breton Island on a 15-acre site filled with wild roses and grasses, the Cape Breton Miners Museum pays tribute to the region's long and rich history of coal mining. It is home to profound stories of miners and their families, and the resource that build Canada,and serves as the fictional location for this story.

Mira River: Flowing past Marion Bridge and Albert Bridge, this storied and scenic river discharges into Mira Bay.

MNA: Irish Word For 'WOMEN'; See 'FIR'.

Mountie: common nick name for a member of the RCMP.

Oireachtas (pl.Oireachtais): [pronounced Oh Rock' Tas] A regional or world championship for traditional Irish-dancing.

Overburden: Material that lies above an area that lends itself to mining, such as the rock and ecosystem that lies above a coal seam.

PEI : Prince Edward island, Canada's smallest province.

Quarterdeck: the main ceremonial reception area aboard ship.

RCAF: Royal Canadian Air Force A vital component of the Canadian Armed Forces.

RCMP: the federal and national police force of Canada. It also provides provincial policing in Nova Scotia,in areas where no local law enforcement agency has been established.

Robbing Pillars: The systematic removal of the coal pillars between rooms or chambers to cause a mine's roof to cave in. Robbing the pillars was one of the most dangerous jobs in the mine, but often forced upon 'bootleg' miners by poverty.

Shearwater: CFB Shearwater, is a Canadian Forces Base located in Shearwater, Nova Scotia on the eastern shore of Halifax Harbour.

Sprag Your Wheels: Slow Down! Miner's argot, derived from a short billet of wood used instead of a brake to lock the wheels of a runaway coal wagon.

Ssgt: Staff Sergeant, a rank in both the RCMP and CBRP between Sergeant and Inspector.

Step-Dancing: The generic term for dance styles in which the footwork is the most important part of the dance.

Sydney: The historic capital of Cape Breton and largest urban center on the island.

Tunnel: an underground passageway, dug through the surrounding soil or rock and enclosed except for entrance and (sometimes) an exit.

VSU : Victim Support Unit, a common element of many police agencies.

YQY: International Airport code for JA Douglas McCurdy Sydney Airport

NOTE: Chapter titles have been adapted from the lyrics of several songs of 'The Men Of The Deeps' a world-famous chorus of retired Cape Breton coal miners who call the Miners Museum home.

OTHER WORKS ON THESE TOPICS:

The reader may be interested in these works; presented without the overlay of fiction:

CHAPTER - 1

"Feis." Wikipedia, Wikimedia Foundation, Retrieved 2 Feb 2018 en.wikipedia.org/wiki/Feis.

"Oireachtas" (Irish Dance)." Wikipedia, Wikimedia Foundation,Retrieved 13 Feb 2018 www.clrg.ie/index.php/en/championships/world-championships.html

The Home of Irish Dancing - Antonio Pacelli,

https://www.antoniopacelli.com/community/blog/.../beginner
s-guide-to-irish-dancing Retrieved 22 Feb 2017

CHAPTER - 2

Reilly Security Systems, reilly1932.com/reilly-security-
systems/projects/airports.html. Retrieved Retrieved 10 Feb
2018

Marine Security Enforcement Team - Fact Sheet - Maritime ...

http://www.ccg-gcc.gc.ca/eng/CCG/Maritime-Security/Fact-
Sheet/MSET Retrieved 12 Feb 2018

Government of Canada, Fisheries and Oceans Canada, 24 June
2013,www.ccg-gcc.gc.ca/eng/CCG/Maritime-Security/Fact-
Sheet/MSET. Retrieved 15 Feb 2018

CHAPTER - 3

Irish Dance FEIS TIPS: Ten Helpful Hints for Competing at
Your First ...The Home of Irish Dancing - Antonio Pacelli,
www.antoniopacelli.com/community/blog Ten Helpful Hints
Retrieved 20 Feb 2018

Basic Guide to Irish Dancing - The Reel Life "Basic Guide to
Irish Dancing." The Reel Life, thereellife.weebly.com/basic-
guide-to-irish-dancing.html. Retrieved 23 Feb 2018

CHAPTER - 6

Morgan, R. J. Rise Again!: the Story of Cape Breton Island.
Breton Books, 2008. Retrieved 26 Feb 2018

Davis, Stephen A., and Stephen A. Davis. Mikmaq. Nimbus Pub., 1997. Retrieved 26 Feb 2018

"Colony of Cape Breton." Wikipedia, Wikimedia Foundation, 24 Mar. 2018, en.wikipedia.org/wiki/Colony_of_Cape_Breton. Retrieved 27 Feb 2018

"Mi'kmaq." Wikipedia, Wikimedia Foundation, en.wikipedia.org/wiki/Mi'kmaq. Retrieved 28 Feb 2018

CHAPTER - 7

Fortress Louisbourg - mysummersnow.com

https://mysummersnow.com/Fortress_Louisbourg.html Retrieved Mar 2018

CHAPTER - 11

Freedom for - Chechnya: The least price of Russian war crimes

https://www.islamicity.org/555/freedom-for-- Chechnya-the-least-price-of-russian-war-crimes/ Retrieved Mar 2018

CHAPTER - 14

Anthem of the Chechnya Republic - YouTube

https://www.youtube.com/watch ?v=o54VjsdTFj8 Retrieved Mar 2018

CHAPTER - 16

Special Weapons And Tactics | SWAT - American Special Ops

"Special Weapons & Tactics | SWAT." American Special Ops, www.americanspecialops.com/special-weapons-and-tactics/. Retrieved

A SWAT operator's entry weapon of PoliceOne

https://www.policeone.com/swat/.../4274548-A-SWAT-operators-entry-weapon-of-CHAPTER - ... \ Retrieved 3 Apr 2018

CHAPTER - 19

Legal Aid Program - Justice

http://www.justice.gc.ca/eng/fund-fina/gov-gouv/aid-aide.html

 Government of Canada, Department of Justice, Electronic Communications, 22 Mar. 2017, www.justice.gc.ca/eng/fund-fina/gov-gouv/aid-aide.html. Retrieved 3 Apr 2018

Canadian Criminal Law/Offences/Kidnapping and Unlawful Confinement." Wikibooks, The Free Textbook Project. 8 Mar 2018, 23:41 UTC. 8 Apr 2018, 17:09 ? title=Canadian_Criminal_Law/Offences/Kidnapping_and_Unl awful_Confinement&oldid=3381962>. Retrieved 7 Apr 18

ABOUT THE AUTHORS

J.F. (Jack) Leahy is a noted writer on naval topics, and is the author of eight books on the subject, and who served with USN Mobile Construction Battalion One at Phu Bai and Danang Vietnam in 1969-70. After completing his graduate education as a civilian, he spent nearly thirty years in the intelligence community and telecommunications industry. Upon retiring in 2000, he first taught at the Ross School of Leadership aand Management at Franklin University in Columbus, Ohio. In 2011, he retired as Associate Vice President for Strategic Planning and Extension Services of the Pontifical College Josephinum, a Roman Catholic seminary also in Columbus, Ohio, where he resides with his wife, Margaret.

M.R. (MaryRegina) Quinn is the proud mother and grandmother of accomplished Irish step-dancers. A retired teacher now residing with her husband, Dennis, near Pottstown PA, her most unusual experience before co-authoring this volume was teaching a future major league baseball player as a second-grader. Whether or not he could stay within the lines when coloring as been lost to antiquity. This is her first book.

www.ingramcontent.com/pod-product-compliance
Lightning Source LLC
Chambersburg PA
CBHW071837020726
47502CB00004B/1405